TALES FROM

The
Catskill Tribune

The Mountains' Premier Source for Fake News

by
JERALD T. MILANICH

the Peppertree Press, LLC
Sarasota, Florida

ISBN: 978-1-61493-702-9
Library of Congress Number: 2020905729
Printed June 2020

To the Catskill Mountains:
people and nature at their finest.

CONTENTS

PREFACE

For more than a decade I've been learning about the Catskill Mountains in upstate New York. My perhaps overactive imagination continues to see a lot of humor in what I've found. When the 2016 presidential campaign added "fake news" and "alternative facts" to America's lexicon, I decided it might be fun to combine the past and the present with alternative facts in a series of Catskill-focused, newspaper-like articles.

Those fake news stories first appeared in an online newspaper that I christened the *Roxbury Tribune*. the *Roxbury Tribune* eventually became the *Catskill Tribune,* which, in turn, became this book.

In some instances, *Catskill Tribune* "reporters" have written follow-ups to stories appearing in this volume. The "editor-in-chief" thought postscripts would be of interest to *Tribune* subscribers—which is how I think of my readers.

This book is a work of fiction in which actual places, historical events, and a few real individuals, some dead and some alive, are mixed with a host of imaginary people and events. President Donald Trump certainly exists, as do the Catskill hamlets of Willow and Breakabeen; gangster Dutch Schultz's real name was indeed Arthur Flegenheimer; and the Hardenburgh Patent is a historical document that was very important in the settlement of the Catskill Mountains in the late eighteenth and nineteenth centuries. I had a great time surrounding those and other people, places, and things with a lot of alternative facts (some would say fiction.)

I hope subscribers will have as much enjoyment reading these tales as I had writing them. There is no place like the Catskills!

1. BEAR CRASHES WEDDING

"I Do's" Quickly Become "I'm Out of Here"

It was a carefully choreographed, early evening "wedding in the round" in a beautiful meadow in the western Catskill Mountains. Guests sat in chairs arranged in circles around a chuppah-like arbor decorated with sacred Tibetan symbols. Concentric rows of chairs were festooned with crepe paper in various colors, the overall design resembling a giant Navajo prayer rug.

Conducting the ceremony was one of the bride's sisters who was a minister of the American Fellowship Church and who recently had received her doctoral degree in anthropological linguistics at SUNY Albany.

The minister had just finished reading poems in Swahili and Oneida (an Iroquoian Indian language) and was about to administer vows to the first bride when a large black bear ambled out of the nearby woods, heading for the table of hot and cold hors d'oeuvres. Bride number 2 saw the bear first and loudly screamed, "Holy s--t! There's a bear!"

In unison the audience stood up, looked at the bear, and began running in the opposite direction. Unfortunately, that direction led to a steep escarpment that sloped down to a rock-strewn stream. People slid, rolled, and stumbled into the cold mountain water. Getting up the bank on the opposite side, however, was more than most guests could manage.

In the meantime, the bear was polishing off a large platter of andouille en croute (pigs-in-a-blanket) faster than you could say Sam's Club. Three of bride number 1's bridesmaids and two of bride number 2's took a stand under the chuppah and were chucking rocks at the bear. One of the five, who had a real potty-mouth, was also loudly spewing invectives.

The bravery of the five women was in large part due to a bottle of Southern Comfort they had imbibed while singing Janis Joplin hits and dressing for the wedding.

The bear had just turned her attention to two trays of smoked salmon when a fist-sized rock knocked over a Sterno can under a chafing dish of prosciutto-wrapped dates, spilling flame down the tablecloth. That and a size 8½ powder-blue Jimmy Choo pump expertly hurled by one of the bridesmaids that struck the bear squarely in the snout convinced bruin it was time to leave.

Many guests eventually returned from the stream, tattered and sharing a host of contusions. Others walked back to town, and nearly a dozen were found later wandering along an adjacent country road, disoriented and thoroughly lost.

The wedding was called off and the two brides-to-be announced they were eloping sometime in the future. They plan to keep all wedding presents received to date.

A year later a check with the two brides revealed that they did indeed elope, but not far. Since they already had their wedding license, they simply checked into a local hotel and the ceremony was performed the next day on the hotel grounds overlooking a beautiful waterfall.

We caught up with the newly married couple in Austin, Texas, where they now live. Both are employed as brokers in a well-known financial firm. The two were eager to relate what had befallen them in the last thirteen months.

"Last fall both of us became pregnant, sharing the same sperm donor. We were careful to get a guy from Manhattan (as opposed to Staten Island or the Bronx). The best thing about our new jobs is that the company provides paid maternity leave for up to six months. You are supposed to sign a form when you are hired, disclosing whether or not you are pregnant at the time (which allows the company to waive the leave), but the ninny in personnel must have thought two married women would never be preggers. HAH!

"As soon as our six-month paid leaves are over, we are moving back to the New York area. Austin, a little blue dot in a sea of deep red, is not bad, but have you ever traveled in the rest of Texas? Forget it.

"Though we don't know the gender of the two kids, we have picked out names that will work for either a boy or a girl: Austin and Joplin. Pretty cool, huh?"

2. PRESIDENT DONALD J. TRUMP VISITS CATSKILLS

Biggest Celebrity in Region Since Jay Gould's Body Toured in 1892

The Catskills' worst-kept secret was revealed Saturday afternoon when President Donald Trump's one day "Make the Catskills Great Again" tour arrived in Roxbury. Earlier the President and his entourage were in Delhi, Delaware County's county seat, where the President delivered a twelve-minute speech to a crowd estimated by local officials at thirty-five people, considerably fewer than the "thousands" mentioned in Fox News television coverage.

Rumors that the President was going to be in the Catskills and perhaps in Roxbury arose several weeks ago when numerous large black SUVs with government license plates were seen around town. Apparently, a Secret Service advance team was checking routes and locations. A separate security detail was in Roxbury vetting backgrounds of local residents deemed suspicious (hundreds of people were on the list).

Last Saturday shortly after noon, President Trump's Marine One helicopter was seen flying northward over Margaretville and Halcottsville before landing in the horse pasture at the end of Scott Greene Road in Roxbury.

Nearly two hours before the helicopter landed, a parade of mud-splattered rental cars carrying reporters arrived at the pasture. The press corps expressed dismay there was no cellular telephone service. A local Scott Greene Road resident who had a Wi-Fi net-work set up around his house agreed to let members of the media sit in his yard for $50 and log on to his connection. Reporters who paid the fee were allowed to use his bathroom for an additional $5; otherwise, the bathroom charge was $10.

To dissuade reporters from peeing in the woods for free, the local resident downloaded from the internet a photograph of a Canadian wolf, which he hung up next to a sign that read, "If you go into the forest, do not feed the many wild coyotes who live there."

As many as sixty people, including media, secret service agents, presidential aides, and a handful of local town officials were on hand to watch the president's helicopter land. President Trump climbed down from his helicopter, saluted two local volunteer firemen, and was quickly led into a waiting SUV. The procession then drove down Scott Greene Road to Kirkside Park. Before the President arrived at the park, copies of his speech were distributed to the media by Kellyanne Conway, counselor to the President. Thinking that Ms. Conway was Ms. Melania Trump, whose photos he had seen online, one of the volunteer firemen asked her to sign his chest. He was es-corted out of the pasture by Secret Service agents.

President Trump's Speech in Kirkside Park

The oral presentation made by the President in the town's park was a short version of the speech handed out by Kellyanne Conway. Likely that was because an Arctic front accompanied by a squall line was passing through the area at the time.

In his speech the President offered several suggestions intended to make Roxbury and the Catskills great again. At the top of the list was cell phone service. Other suggestions included a pizza palace that delivered, a KFC (especially one that delivered), a McDonalds (also delivery), and reduction of regulations so small businesses could receive a liquor license from the state in only six to nine months, not the two to three years it presently takes. In an off-the-cuff remark, President Trump hinted he was interested in a Trump Hotel and Ski Center in the Catskills. He noted, "I bet I could get all the necessary permits in a few months."

Officials from Margaretville, already miffed that their town was not on the President's itinerary, grew even angrier when the President referred to their village as "the Roxbury suburb of Margaritaville."

Following his speech, the President and his immediate entourage returned to the horse pasture and the waiting helicopter. The media and security entourage headed north in cars and SUVs, intent on arriving in Prattsville before the President landed there and delivered his third and final speech of the day.

One Margaretville town official was heard telling a *Christian Science Monitor* reporter that "unlike Roxbury, Prattsville has cell service and so do we."

A local photographer well-known for her images of Catskill weddings may have taken the photograph of a lifetime on Saturday immediately after the President disembarked from Marine One in Roxbury.

Walking through the pasture on the way to his waiting SUV, the president stepped in a clump of dried and partially frozen horse manure. While a Secret Service agent held his left arm, the President violently shook his right foot to dislodge the manure from his shoe. The clump flew forward about ten feet and hit aide Kellyanne Conway in the back.

Believing the manure was thrown by one of the members of the media, Ms. Conway turned around and made an obscene hand gesture at the New York Times reporter. At that moment the photographer, hired as a stringer by the Catskill Mountain News, snapped a digital image of Ms. Conway who appeared to be gesturing at the President.

The photograph was picked up by national and international news sources and appeared in the Sunday morning editions of more than 130 United States and foreign newspapers. Saturday Night Live has already contacted the photographer about using the photograph in an upcoming sketch.

3. TROUBLING VIEW OF CELEBRATED NATURALIST JOHN BURROUGHS EMERGES FROM DIARIES

Legacy of Catskills Icon under Siege

Four diaries, two kept by Ursula North, the wife of John Burroughs, and two by Clara Barrus, a long-time Burroughs acquaintance, are providing historians with a revisionist perspective on Roxbury's famed native son. Ms. Barrus was a long-time admirer and close friend of Burroughs who moved in with him when he returned to live in Roxbury following the death of his wife in 1917.

The hand-written diaries, all expensive leather-bound volumes, were found with other books in a cupboard in a farmhouse attic on Hardscrabble Road in Roxbury. Based on entries in the diaries, some authorities now believe Burroughs became a whiskey-swilling reprobate who, after he met Barrus in 1901, likely never wrote another word. Most of his earlier work might actually have been written by Ursula North, while either North or Barrus or a combination of the two wrote under Burroughs' name after 1901. The relationship between North and Barrus is not clear.

Burroughs, who died in 1921 in Ohio, lived out the last years of his life at Woodchuck Lodge, a rural Roxbury retreat where it was hoped his alcohol-fueled shenanigans might escape public scrutiny. According to one diary entry, he had been sent to Ohio to seek medical treatment for his problem when he died while aboard a train headed west.

Woodchuck Lodge and Burroughs' nearby grave have become shrines to ecologists, naturalists, and other Burroughs aficionados. More than twenty books and numerous articles attributed to him are still widely read today.

Shockingly, diary entries call into question that entire literary oeuvre. Everything attributed to him may have been written by one or the other or both of the two women. The diaries intimate that Burroughs was incapacitated by drink most of the time.

Rather than a gentle man of nature, Burroughs is portrayed in the diaries as a barely functioning alcoholic. In his last years he was incapable of seeing to his personal hygiene, hence, his disheveled appearance in photographs. When drinking, he had a terrible temper and was abusive to both women. His repeated bouts of alcohol-related illnesses led his neighbors on Hardscrabble Road to refer to Woodchuck Lodge as Upchuck Lodge.

Why did North and Barrus choose to attribute their own ideas, observations, and writings to Burroughs? There are hints in the diaries. In the nineteenth and early twentieth centuries, women were not afforded opportunities for recognition as biologists or naturalists.

In Burroughs the women found an individual who appeared to the public both as a child-like outdoorsman and an eccentric scientist, a combination that sold books and magazines. Publishers were eager to put in print anything said to be written by him. Burroughs' alcoholism left him unaware of much that was occurring around him and so gave the two women a free hand to exercise their own intellect and publish under his name.

One entry from 1914 made after Burroughs met Henry Ford

and Thomas Edison reads, "JB muttered, who in hell are those two birds? How come they didn't want a drink?" Later he had no remembrance of the meeting.

Burroughs was never allowed to drive the car Henry Ford gave him, though he was posed in it for photographs. The two women also posed with him for other photographs, all of which were made into postcards and sold to raise household money. Literally hundreds of the postcards still exist today with many offered for sale on eBay.

According to the diaries, Burroughs' behavior at times was bizarre. More than once he wandered into the woods near Woodchuck Lodge and became lost. Neighbors were recruited to form search parties. The ditty, "How much booze can a woodchuck use," became a local joke. Often searchers found Burroughs asleep in a forest glade scratched and smeared with deer scat.

According to one diary, at the time of the full moon, Burroughs would tie his long beard up on top of his head, remove his clothes, and run through pastures, stopping to point his bare buttocks at the moon and howl like a wolf. Residents on Hardscrabble Road referred to these incidents as "mooning," a term picked up by Roxbury school kids and now known the world over. It may be Burroughs' most lasting legacy.

4. CELL PHONE SCAMMERS HIT HALCOTTSVILLE, ROXBURY, AND MARGARETVILLE

Starved for reliable mobile phone service, a number of local Catskill residents fell hard for a "too good to be true" scheme. On Tuesday and Wednesday of last week three pleasantly coifed women estimated to be in their late twenties or early thirties went door-to-door selling what was purported to be cell phone access.

For $250 dollars (cash only), buyers received a red baseball-type hat with a built-in antenna that promised to pick up cell phone service anywhere in the United States. The cost included a mobile smart phone that was to be mailed to each purchaser within two working days. None of the phones have been received.

According to several people that fell for the scheme, each phone was purported to come loaded with two apps. One was for meeting young local singles, while the second provided direct access to Roxbury and Margaretville liquor stores and guaranteed free home delivery.

Buyers also were told that fifteen percent of each purchase would be donated to a local food bank. The slogan "MAKE AMERICA——EAT AGAIN" was emblazoned on the front of each China-made antenna cap.

Law enforcement authorities were alerted when one of the saleswomen knocked on the door of a Roxbury Run townhouse unit.

The owner immediately recognized that the two "young local singles" portrayed on the brochure he was handed were actually images of Judy Garland from a 1954 A Star is Born movie poster (James Mason was cropped) and RuPaul as portrayed in an advertisement for the low budget film Star Booty III: Star Booty's Revenge popular in Atlanta movie houses in the mid-1980s.

To date thirty-five people have come forward to admit they had paid the $250 subscription fee. There have been no recent sightings of the three women who likely have moved on to one of the many dead cell phone zones on Route 28 between Fleischmanns and West Hurley.

5. MASSIVE POLICE RAID ROILS CATSKILL RESIDENTS

Sunday morning at 4 a.m. combined Homeland Security, FBI, and state law enforcement agents raided a local Roxbury hotel. According to neighbors who watched the whole operation unfold, there were at least forty agents, a bomb disposal unit, and a portable food truck serving coffee and pastries. The truck and its crew were leased for the night from a local company.

By the time the raid began, nearly everyone in town was aware of what was unfolding and many residents were sitting on their porches bundled up in blankets to watch. One bar/restaurant opened at 3:30 a.m. to serve onlookers.

Events leading up to the hastily planned raid began only hours earlier in a bar in Arkville. At about 5 p.m. Albert Kado, a Rotarian from Andes who owns a gun shop, stopped in for a quick drink. There he met Wanda Devo, vice president of public relations for the Association of Muslin Cloth Manufacturers. Ms. Devo was staying at a Roxbury hotel while negotiating a retreat for company executives and was checking out bars and restaurants and other amenities in the area. It was love at first sight. Kado and Devo moved to a quiet corner table to talk.

Kado and Devo began to exchange stories about their lives: tales of guns, muslin cloth, and the terrors of life under the new administration in Washington. By chance an employee of the New York City Department of Conservation happened to sit down nearby. He caught a few words of the Devo-Kado conversation just as the police scanner app on his smart phone picked up an APB (All-Points Bulletin) about two possible Al-Qaida terrorists. The two were believed to have had flown into Albany after entering the country via an international flight to Atlanta.

It took the NYCDC employee only a minute to put it all together: guns, Muslims, terrorists. Though badly shaken, he called the Department of Homeland Security hot line. In minutes federal, state, and local law enforcement agencies were alerted that the fugitive terrorists had surfaced.

A call to the bar in Arkville quickly turned up Ms. Devo's name on a credit card receipt. In less than ten minutes, authorities traced her to the hotel where she was staying in the Mae West suite. An astute agent then asked for the names of other guests and found that a Mr. Albert Kado (which the agent discerned was an alias for Al Qaeda) had recently checked into Room 4.

By 2 a.m. agents had set up a perimeter and began a clandestine advance on the hotel. The plan called for simultaneous forced entries on Room 4 and the Mae West Suite at 4 a.m.

That is when things began to fall apart. In the dark, Team A misread a room number and broke down the door of Room 9 and found it empty. Team B also found the Mae West Suite to be unoccupied. As it turned out the suspects were together in Room 4.

On entering the Mae West Suite, Team B could not take their eyes off the décor and accoutrements, including a man's bathrobe with a huge Styrofoam banana in the pocket. A rookie FBI agent happened to glance up and see his reflection in the mirror above the round bed. Thinking it was a Ninja Radical Islamic Terrorist, he drew his Glock and fired a single round that shattered the mirror and traveled up through the ceiling and the roof.

By chance, light from the moon shining down through the new hole illuminated a crystal crucifix left by Ms. Devo on the bedstand.

Several of the more religious agents knelt and were crossing themselves when the hotel owners walked in to survey damage. They told this reporter that following the incident, they planned to redecorate the room using an "our Lady of Fatima shrine" motif, including a life-size, walk-in Plexiglas crucifix.

By 6 a.m. pastries and coffee were gone and the law enforcement personnel had departed.

6. BLACK ICE THWARTS LOCAL VIGILANTES

Four unemployed local residents who unwisely decided to take the law into their own hands two days ago were stopped by nature while traveling at a high rate of speed on Route 30 between Roxbury and Grand Gorge. Three of the men, all Andes residents, were transported by helicopter to an Albany hospital. The fourth, John Biery, was taken to rehab.

The ill-thought-out saga began at a convenience store about 5 p.m. when Mr. Biery went in to buy a liter of Mountain Dew and a large bag of Doritos. He later told first responders that he had spent the day at home drinking most of a case of Pabst, smoking marijuana, and binge-watching the first five seasons of The Americans recorded on a boxed set of DVDs he had found at the Middletown Transfer Station. The show, about Russian sleeper agents posing as Americans, recently began its sixth season on television.

Thinking he needed to shape up before his wife returned from work, Mr. Biery rode his lawn mower into downtown Roxbury in a search of soda and snacks. Once in the store Mr. Biery observed a well-dressed couple buying a copy of the New York Times newspaper. The man carried a bottle of vodka just purchased in town. When the woman told the sales clerk that they were rushing to their daughter's in Grand Gorge. Mr. Biery thought the woman had said, "We're Russian and going to our dacha in Grand Gorge." That, the vodka, and the New York Times left no doubt in Mr. Biery's mind that standing before him were two godless, Russian Communist sleeper agents.

Borrowing the store phone, Biery called a bar in Margaretville where three friends were fraternizing. The three grabbed their deer rifles, a bottle of maple-flavored whiskey, and jumped into their well-used Willys Jeep. Arriving in Roxbury, they loaded up Mr. Biery, what was left of the Doritos, the unopened Mountain Dew, and four six-packs of Genesee beer. The store clerk reported that the four men then spent about twenty minutes drinking and arguing about who got to sit in the front seat of the Willys.

Intent on driving to Grand Gorge, locating the dacha, and making a citizen's arrest of the family of sleeper agents, the four departed Roxbury at a high rate of speed. North of the Roxbury Transfer Station, they hit a patch of black ice, slid into the rock cliff on the left, did a 270-degree skid, and ended up in the headwaters of the East Branch whereupon Mr. Bier vomited copiously on his companions.

First responders arrived, hosed down the interior of the vehicle and its occupants, wrapped them in blankets, and called in a medivac helicopter that flew the men from the scene. The Grand Gorge family remains unidentified.

7. EXCLUSIVE *CATSKILL TRIBUNE* INTERVIEW WITH WOMAN WHO SHOT UP HOME

It was the talk of the Catskills. A woman living on a gravel road in Montgomery Hollow in the northwestern Catskills had "gone berserk" with shotgun in hand. What caused her to do it? This reporter set out to find her and gain an interview.

I located the woman and she consented to speak with me. She was not a Catskill native. Like many other people living in the area, she had moved from New York City, having earned an MBA degree from a prestigious business school. After nearly a decade of eighteen-hour days at an investment firm and after banking a fortune by Catskill standards, she decided to give up her Hampton weekends for what she hoped was a less demanding life, one which allowed time to write poetry, raise chickens, and enjoy the beauty around her.

Here is her story in her own words.

"I woke up Saturday morning just after dawn. The chickens were raising hell in the coop in the backyard. I knew what was happening, so I jumped out of bed, grabbed my double-barreled shotgun, and went to find my shoes. By the time I got there, a mink or fox had killed six laying hens and broken about a dozen eggs.

"About ten o'clock, I was working on another poem for my book:

Catskill Idylls. I love writing on the MacBook Air I had bought myself for Christmas. Just then the electricity blipped. It was off just long enough to cause all the clocks to blink. I got up and reset them all.

"An hour and a half later the same thing happened and I reset them again. Then it happened a third time.

"When it happened a fourth time, I lost it. I picked up the shotgun, blasted two clocks, reloaded, and took out the oven clock and then the one on the microwave. Then the TV, the MacBook Air, and the framed photos on the walls. Then the windows. When I ran out of shells, I just went outside and laid down.

"That's where the state trooper found me—in the driveway with the six dead chickens. He asked if I was involved in Santeria or Voodoo or anything like that and I said, "No, I wasn't making any offerings. I was just resting and writing poetry in my head." He said OK and left. I'm moving back to NYC. It's too stressful here."

8. FLEISCHMANNS MEETING ENERGIZES TOWN

Less than a month ago Jonathan Crocker moved to the small burg of Fleischmanns from the San Francisco Bay area. He hinted he might make major investments in the Catskill Mountain town and proposed that city officials hold a charrette, hire a facilitator, and come up with a plan for the town's future. The plan drew blank stares from many of the residents who thought a charrette was something that women used to hold their hair.

But Crocker persisted and the town agreed to match the $2000 Crocker said he would put up of his own money to organize two charrettes (town meetings) and hire a facilitator (a moderator) to help channel discussions. The $4000 was to be paid to a San Francisco firm called Meetings "R" Us. The initial charrette held last week is likely the town's last.

After asking all those present at the meeting to introduce themselves and speak about their interests in bettering Fleischmanns, the facilitator (Lila Hall) began writing objectives for discussion on a whiteboard propped on an easel.

Item 1 was to suggest a new name for the town. The name Fleischmanns was written on the board with a large red slash drawn through it. Audience members were aghast. Hall told them that people equated Fleischmanns with yeast and yeast with an infection associated with women's problems. "You need a new name," she insisted.

At that point a central school ninth grader sitting in the back of the room stood up and told the assembled citizens that she had googled both Mr. Crocker and Ms. Hall and discovered they were married. The student further reported that Meetings "R" Us had outstanding arrest warrants in seven states from California to New York.

One attendee, who still did not understand what a charrette was and thought a facilitator was his first wife who supplied his drugs, threw a folding chair. A small riot erupted during which time Crocker and Hall exited the building headed toward Maine.

9. BATTLE OF SHACKSVILLE REENACTMENT CANCELED

Following a chaotic dress rehearsal and on the advice of numerous attorneys, members of the local historical society have called off next Saturday's commemoration of the 1845 Battle of Shacksville.

The original Shacksville skirmish took place during the mid-nineteenth century Anti-Rent War when a local sheriff and posse confronted and arrested several Roxbury men accused of acts of civil disobedience and physical assault. They and other protestors—known as Down-Renters—opposed the rents they were forced to pay wealthy landowners, the Up-Renters.

The arrests took place in the small hamlet then known as Shacksville, located south of Roxbury along the East Branch of the Delaware River near the Briggs Road Bridge, in the area later called Brookdale.

According to Jay Gould's 1856 book History of Delaware County, the Down-Renter protestors disguised themselves as Indians, wearing "A calico dress ... encircled around the waist by a belt usually ornamented with a profusion of tassels and other fantastic ornaments, together with the implements of warfare ... of an artificial Indian." Masks made of sheepskin completed the outfits.

Ultimately the efforts of the Down-Renters resulted in the dissolution of the feudal-like system that had persisted in the Catskills since the late 18th century. Before state laws were enacted to end the rents, one Up-Renter was shot and killed and another was tarred and feathered. A number of Down-Renters were arrested and imprisoned.

Fortunately, last week's rehearsal, overseen and choreographed by the local State University of New York-New Paltz chapter of the Society for Creative Anachronism (SCA), did not result in any deaths. However, there were numerous injuries including a broken collar bone, broken arm, numerous cuts and contusions, and many bruised egos.

The rehearsal, held in a fallow agricultural field adjacent to Briggs Road, featured two local associations whose members agreed to play roles in the conflict. As luck would have it, the Catskills Men's Chorus and the Western Catskills Bar Association both showed up thinking they were to portray the Down-Renters. Neither group wanted to be greedy landlords.

While negotiations took place, the Society for Creative Anachronism began passing out plastic cups of mead to participants. In short order what had been a gentlemanly discussion turned into insults and then violence.

One attorney told a Men's Chorus member that his calico costume made him look like he should be doing a do-si-do at an Alabama square dance. He also made fun of the man's mask, calling it something a drag queen would wear in a Mardi Gras parade. The chorus member retorted that the attorney's whitish dress made him look like the Grand Wizard of the Ku Klux Klan.

The attorney, a dues-paying member of the American Civil Liberties Union, took umbrage at the remark and hit the singer with the handle of a wooden pitchfork. Shoving and then fisticuffs broke out all over the field.

It took nearly an hour to calm the situation. Amid a number of threats of lawsuits, the rehearsal was called off, as was next week's reenactment.

This reporter spoke to a member of the Society for Creative Anachronism about the mead that seemed to be the catalyst for the violence. The woman, a SUNY sophomore whose SCA persona is Dowager of Libations said that the venerable drink was made using an old recipe from "The Canterbury Tales or something like that" and consisted of one-part honey, a little maple syrup flavoring, and four parts Everclear 190 proof grain alcohol.

"These old guys are wimps," she noted. "Before a joust, most of us have eight or ten mead Jell-O shots and nothing like this ever happens."

10. ROXIT? NEWLY DISCOVERED COLONIAL DOCUMENT CHARTS NEW FUTURE FOR CATSKILL TOWN

Will the Town of Roxbury secede from New York State and join Great Britain? Recent polls commissioned by business owners suggest that what only weeks ago was a far-fetched plan may be closer—much closer—to reality.

This extraordinary turn of events began in the fall when students at the Central School began researching the history of Roxbury as a class project. They decided to focus on the Hardenburgh or "Great" Patent, a 1707 document that recorded the "purchase" from Native Americans of approximately two million acres of land between the Hudson and Delaware Rivers. Johannes Hardenburgh, who negotiated the deal, was given approval for the transaction from Anne, Queen of England, Scotland, and Ireland.

The lands later were divided into Great Lots that were subdivided into smaller tracts. By 1750 ownership of lots was held by individuals in Britain and the American colonies, though little settlement had occurred. Following the 1783 signing of the Treaty of Paris that ended the Revolutionary War and granted America's independence, farmers began to move onto Patent lands, though they had to pay rent to the owners.

The Central School students thought it instructive to locate the original Patent and the document in which Queen Anne gave her approval. Their search has changed history.

Found attached to the Queen's authorizing signature was a letter written in her own hand that specified that Great Lot 47 of the Patent would forever remain a part of Great Britain and could not be "sold, ceded, or otherwise transferred" by subsequent "treaty, sale, or gift." Exactly why Great Lot 47 was chosen is not known, but a love interest of Queen Ann is suspected.

Maps indicate that Great Lot 47 encompasses the modern town of Roxbury. The class consulted a local attorney and officials in several New York State agencies, as well as an English barrister specializing in Pre-Revolutionary War land claims. All agreed that it was illegal for Great Lot 47 to have been included in lands transferred to the United States of America as part of the Treaty of Paris. Roxbury is a part of Great Britain, or, as the English attorney put it, "Roxbury is as Brit as Bonny Prince Charles."

Roxbury residents and officials at first pooh-poohed the claim. But as word spread individuals began to ask questions. If we are British citizens can we avoid paying taxes to the Internal Revenue Service? How about New York State? Might the Queen or, better, Prince Harry visit? Almost overnight a ground swell of support arose for a "Roxit:" leaving the United States for Great Britain.

Some Roxbury residents complained that they would have to learn to drive on the right-hand side of the road. They were shouted down by others who noted local people already drive pretty much however they want.

With that concern allayed, many have embraced Roxit, including the business community. Local visionaries foresee a Ye Olde Spirits Shoppe, a drive-through Fish and Chips emporium, and a Scottish-style haggis food truck that also serves Scotch whiskey.

Central School students are enthused about changing the name of their sports teams to Beefeaters, honoring the Queen of England's palace guard. They also have begun a cricket team. Two Roxbury residents have inquired about serving as Roxbury's consular officials in Ireland.

A major stimulus for accepting Roxit came last week when British Telecommunications promised to bring cellular phone service to Roxbury when the town joins Great Britain.

After a straw poll indicated more than seventy-five percent of residents supported Roxit, the town council declared a plebiscite be held on May 29, a Bank Holiday in the UK, to vote on the issue. Under laws that existed at the time of the original Hardenburgh Patent, everyone who owns property in Roxbury (landsmen)—not just registered voters—will be allowed to cast a ballot.

11. ROXIT VOTE NEARS; TOWN PROPERTY OWNERS TALK OF NOTHING ELSE

Neighboring Towns Are Covetous

With the plebiscite to decide whether or not Roxbury secedes from the United States of America only days away, local residents are consumed by the gravity of the situation. Discussions, arguments, and even an occasional fist fight have divided the town into two factions.

Those opting to remain with the United States have been sporting T-shirts reading on the front WE'RE WITH THE US in red, white, and blue letters. On the back of the shirts in even larger font are the letters "WWUS." The acronym has led those favoring succession to call people in the opposing camp Wusses, hence the fisticuffs.

Informal polls suggest the "We're with the United States" group is outnumbered at least four to one. The promise of no more bed taxes, county taxes, school taxes, and state and federal income taxes continues to entice a large segment of property owners to vote to join the United Kingdom.

The vote will be held on May 29 (a UK bank holiday and the day Memorial Day is celebrated this year in the United States).

Other towns in Delaware and adjacent counties have asked their own central school students to research the Hardenburgh Patent to see if they, too, might be eligible to join the UK.

Officials in the village of Margaretville in Middletown are

concerned that if Roxbury votes to join the United Kingdom, tourists will flock to businesses there, leaving Margaretville adrift. One idea gaining steam is to change the name of the town to Margaritaville to garner attention. An ad hoc committee of Margaretville business leaders and residents issued the following statement:

It is time for the village of Margaretville to bite the bullet and do what we should have done years ago: change the name of our village to Margaritaville. A poll of our residents shows that absolutely no one knows the Margaret for whom our town was named, while over ninety percent are familiar with margaritas.

Such a name change will bring a younger generation to our village, as well as tourists hoping to find an ambience like that in Key West, Florida. We need to make a bold move to get our piece of the economic pie.

A telephone call to Jimmy Buffet's publicist elicited this response: "We'd love a Margaritaville in upstate New York. Is that far from New York City? I'm certain Jimmy would be thrilled to go up there and sing and sell some of his signature flip flops. It doesn't get cold there, does it?"

In anticipation of the name change, one local Margaretville business is adding sponge cake to its repertoire of cheeses, while another is including alcohol resistant blenders in her store's inventory of home goods. The price of tequila in stores in Roxbury and Margaretville has risen, a reflection of increased demand.

One Albany television station carried a forty-second news item about the impending Roxit vote, which thus far has not drawn attention outside Delaware County. That may change if the vote passes and Roxbury officials issue the already drafted "Declaration of Dependence." The succinct Declaration states the town is seceding from the United States and joining the United Kingdom.

12. ROXBURY VOTES TO JOIN UK; FOX NEWS LABELS MOVE "STENCH OF INFAMY"

President Trump Threatens Retaliation in Early Morning Tweet

In a historic vote on Monday of this week (a UK bank holiday) property owners in the town of Roxbury in the Catskill Mountains voted overwhelmingly to secede from the United States of America and become a part of the United Kington.

The vote was 312 for secession and 37 against. Immediately following the counting of ballots at the Roxbury fire station, town officials set about emailing a "Declaration of Dependence" to governmental agencies in Delhi, NY; Albany; the White House; and the English parliament in London.

The document indicates that the town is leaving the United States and becoming a part of the United Kingdom; it also lays out the legal basis for succession.

The transmission of the unprecedented document was delayed several hours while officials tried to find the proper email addresses. A sixth-grade technology class at the Roxbury Central School assisted in the process.

Roxbury residents have flocked to the streets to celebrate. One local bar and restaurant is featuring a "Freedom Meal" consisting of well-done roast beef, mushy peas, and beans on toast, topped off with a Pimm's Cup. Posters of Her Majesty the Queen and recently retired Prince

Philip have been affixed to both the men's and women's bathroom walls in another eatery.

Tomorrow from 4 to 6 p.m. a local arts group is offering lessons on how to curtsy. Music will be provided by an accordionist who promises to play God Save the Queen.

As soon as news of the secession vote reached the world beyond Roxbury, responses were registered on television and social media. Fox News, in an on-air editorial, referred to the action as having the "stench of infamy." One Fox newscaster proposed that the way to put down the rebellion was to cut off the town's cellular phone service. The suggestion elicited a collective guffaw from Roxbury residents.

President Donald Trump, who likely was watching Fox News, issued the following tweet at 4:22 a.m. Tuesday morning: "We kicked their Brit butts in the 1860s and we can do it again. Cuomo ought to send in the troops."

Three hours later, Sarah Huckabee Sanders, the White House press secretary, released a statement clarifying the President's remarks. She stated the President was aware it was the Civil War that took place in the 1860s and that the War of Independence fought against Great Britain was nearly a century earlier. Asked by reporters if she had actually talked to the President, she indicated she had not.

Alarm that troops might actually march into Roxbury has led residents to organize. Local artists have designed a flag based on the famed, "DON'T TREAD ON ME" rattlesnake banner of the American Revolution. Roxbury's "battle flag" features a fierce-looking groundhog with the slogan "DON'T RUN ME OVER."

The Catskill Men's Chorus graciously offered to design uniforms for the Roxbury Militia, members of which were drafted from the Roxbury volunteer fire department. Chorus members selected an ensemble from the 1938 Errol Flynn movie, Robin Hood: lime green tights with a brown jerkin, and a peculiar hat. Thus far fire department members have refused to even consider wearing the uniform.

Grand Gorge firemen have joined the militia en masse and have been cleaning and oiling rifles. One fireman observed: "What fun! And it's not even hunting season."

A call has gone out to inventory Roxbury's food supplies, in case foreign troops blockade the town. Thus far, the following items have been reported: more than two tons of frozen venison; 892 pounds of other frozen meats (primarily lamb, beef, and pork, but including squirrel); and 722 pounds of unknown frozen items (because the names written on the packages could not be read). There are nearly 500 pounds of seasonal vegetables (mainly carrots and broccoli); over 900 frozen pizzas; and 4,567 gallons of maple syrup. There also are significant amounts of locally produced soap and honey.

Recognizing the possibility of shortages, the local convenience store raised the prices of gasoline and Mountain Dew.

Some residents misunderstood the request related to stored supplies. One hundred-twenty-one people reported stashes of "medical" marijuana and twenty-two listed badminton sets that had never been used. There also were a number of Christmas, Easter, and Halloween inflatable plastic yard decorations most of which had multiple holes from air rifles and could not be used unless patched.

The entire Roxbury community is hunkered down and waiting to see what happens next.

13. THE LATEST ON ROXIT

Still Another Email Glitch

Last week town officials emailed their "Declaration of Dependence" to county, state, federal, and UK governmental bodies, but have received no responses. Suspecting a computer error, students from the local school's fifth grade technology class were called in to examine the town's email setup.

The students quickly discovered that the emails that were supposed to be sent to Delhi, Albany, the White House, and the British Parliament had never actually gone out. The emails were in an email "draft" file; someone had neglected to click the Send button. They have now been dispatched. Town officials promised to take email lessons.

In the meanwhile, townspeople are enjoying their liminal status as people without a country—no longer United States citizens and not yet members of the British Empire. A euphoria reigns in town, a feeling of community and celebration almost equal to that experienced at the annual Roxbury Halloween parade.

The town's battle flag—a fierce-looking groundhog and the slogan "DON'T RUN ME OVER"—has been raised at multiple locales around town.

Uniforms made for the town militia, members of which were recruited from among the volunteer firemen, are being reused by local thespians in Margaretville. You will remember that the Catskill

Men's Chorus had designed uniforms based on those worn by Robin Hood and his merry men in the 1938 Errol Flynn movie. However, the militia members refused to wear the outfits.

The Catskill Men's Chorus graciously designed new uniforms. Deriving their muse from the latest west coast fashion trend, the chorus announced that both male and female militia members will be attired in red one-piece rompers. A spokesperson for the Chorus noted "the red rompers will look great with red fire hats and black rubber boots." As yet there has been no response from the militia.

14. BRIT BARRISTERS BURST ROXBURY'S BALLOON

A month of dreaming about what might have been has ended. Roxbury will remain a part of the United States of America. The town's flirtation with Great Britain is over.

The news was conveyed to Roxbury town officials on Monday, June 26, by diplomats from the British Consulate in New York City who personally drove to Roxbury. They explained the legal and historical issues that negated the addendum to the Hardenburgh or "Great" Patent of 1707 that had been cited as the legal basis for Roxbury's being a part of the British Empire.

The diplomats explained that the addendum to the Hardenburgh Patent was nullified by an appendix to the Treaty of Ghent agreed to by Great Britain and France on December 24, 1814. The treaty, ratified by the United States on February 17, 1815, ended what is known in the United States as the War of 1812, a conflict between the United States and Great Britain. Fighting in the United States, however, continued into early 1815 because it took two months for news of the pact to cross the Atlantic Ocean.

The Ghent treaty appendix specifically addressed the issue of lingering French and British claims on United States lands east of the Mississippi River. Both countries agreed to relinquish all such claims "in perpetuity." Roxbury's claim to membership in the United Kingdom actually ended just over a century after the Hardenburgh Patent was issued.

Many Roxbury residents said they had enjoyed the month-long tax holiday, but were ready to take up their old lives as residents of the United States.

15. TWO-DAY TAKEOVER OF LOCAL RADIO STATION ENDS AMICABLY

Following a Saturday afternoon production meeting at Roxbury's local radio station a disgruntled program host locked herself in the station to protest an increase in country music shows to the detriment of golden oldie programing. For forty-eight straight hours she broadcast Ronnie Milsap's 1985 hit song, Lost in the Fifties Tonight, over and over and over.

Ironically, the song was a Number 1 hit on the Billboard Hot Country Singles & Tracks and never ranked highly on the Pop Music charts.

Supporters of the protest estimate that the four-minute-long song played at least 700 times during the forty-eight hours.

One supporter tried to fly a small drone through an open second-floor window at the radio station to deliver a ham sandwich and a bottle of locally distilled vodka to the activist. The drone, however, dropped both items as it approached the station.

As luck would have it, Wilma Longacre was wheeling her laundry to the Roxbury laundromat when both the bottle and sandwich landed safely on a blue Victoria's Secret baby doll nightie atop her clothes bag.

According to onlookers, Ms. Longacre took one look at her good fortune, raised her eyes and said, "Thank you, Lord," then turned around and headed back home with her clothes and lunch.

The protesting golden oldie advocate emerged from the station about 5 p.m. Monday evening to great acclaim from her supporters.

Station officials announced that during the two days of the protest, the station had received the highest listenership in the station's history.

16. TREE HACKERS, NOT RUSSIAN HACKERS

A review of the one-sided Roxit vote that took place more than a month ago in the town of Roxbury has led nearly a dozen residents to demand an investigation into possible foreign intervention in the election.

The issue arose when several local people noted that just before the vote, a number of white sheets of paper mounted on red posterboard were found placed in store windows around town. Each was entitled BÛCHERONNE and contained four paragraphs of text in a foreign language. What appeared to be a rune or satanic symbol in the form of a peculiar X was printed on each placard. The disgruntled residents decided the notices were fake news exhorting local people to "butcher" or "kill" Roxit, that is, vote against it. It was surmised the notices could be Russian in origin.

Students from the central school were asked to translate the notices and quickly dispelled those fantasies. They pointed out that Bûcheronne was a French word meaning female lumberjack and that the notices were in French and contained information about joining a women's hockey team of that name in Vermont. Many of the team's players were of French-Canadian descent, hence, the name and language.

The X turned out to be crossed hockey sticks.

Thus far, this reporter has identified only one Roxbury resident who applied to join the team. The application of the person, a local attorney and well-known hockey fan, was denied. The basis of the denial was (1) the barrister is a lousy hockey player and, (2) he is male.

17. NEWS FROM AROUND THE REGION

The hullabaloo that ensued when a local congressman took credit for bringing a uranium mine and several hundred high-paying jobs to Ulster County in the Catskills quickly faded last week.

In a phone call to officials at the United States Department of Energy, this reporter was assured there is no uranium mine planned for our region. One official, who asked that his name not be used, said, "That G-- d--- idiot (the congressman) was too busy fussing with his hair and misunderstood comments made by a lobbyist for immigration control."

The lobbyist's oral reference actually was to a Romanian mime scheduled to appear at the library in Phoenicia, not a uranium mine. The Romanian's show was canceled when the performer was not allowed to enter the United States. Department of State officials had denied the man's entry visa application, claiming he likely was a refugee who would have overstayed his visa.

Changes Afoot in Bovina and Roxbury

A "History of Cow Brands Museum" is expected to open in Bovina in several weeks. Christian Potok, a self-proclaimed cowboy from Queens in New York City, is bankrolling the project, which is likely to hire several local residents. By fall Mr. Potok intends to add an oyster bar to the facility, providing more employment opportunities.

In an interview with this newspaper, Mr. Potok stated that his lifelong dream is to run a museum to display his collection of cow brands. "I have hundreds of photographs of brands and actual branding irons from nearly thirty states. I selected Bovina for the museum, because I am certain that a town with that name will draw huge crowds of local residents and tourists. Who wouldn't want to see photos of cows and brands?"

The oyster bar will feature fresh sea food brought in every other week from the panhandle coast of Florida. The restaurant will open in the late spring when Mr. Potok anticipates receiving a state liquor license.

Mr. Potok, who told this reporter he made a small fortune flipping houses in south Florida, wants to establish ties with local public schools and the Delaware Tourist Agency. "I want to give back to the local community for their support of my museum."

Radio Station Changes

Roxbury's local radio station has announced several new programs expected to air this spring.

"Samba for Sissies" at 10 a.m. on Sunday mornings features Carmen Lamão, who offers dance lessons geared to those too frightened or clumsy to hit the dance floor. "I realize it is difficult to teach dancing over the radio, but while living in Costa Rica I originated a method. One sits on a clothes dryer and turns both it and the radio on high. Thanks to the rhythm of the shaking, students can learn to move their hips in no time at all. Future lessons teach listeners to stand and shake, while placing only one hand on the dryer. Then it is a small step from the laundry room to the dance floor."

"Teed Up and Teed Off," scheduled for 11 p.m. on Monday nights will feature conversations with local personalities about golf, life in the Catskills, presidential politics, and local restaurants (or lack thereof). According to the show's host, "We hope to recruit interviewees just before show time from local Roxbury hot spots and then solicit their opinions on the air."

"Real Time in an Alternate Universe" on Thursday afternoons at 4 p.m. promises to entertain listeners with stories of weird Catskill experiences and the many remarkable and unique people who once lived here. Tales of swamp apes, yeti, ephemeral spirits, and the famed Catskill transgender huntress of Delaware County, Lucy Ann/ Joseph Israel Lobdel, will be offered.

"Farm to Table and Back Again: The Second Harvest" will air at 11:30 a.m. just before the lunch hour each day. Our experts will discuss planting, growing, harvesting, preparing, cooking, and eating local plants, animals, and even slugs. Nothing is too large or too small to escape the rapacious interests of our food mavens, who represent the realm of diets from Atkins to Keto to Paleo. What makes this show unique is that hosts take food one step further, focusing on composting leftover scraps and night soil to fertilize plants, feed animals, and attract shell-less gastropods.

"Music That You've Never Experienced" is a thirty-minute Friday evening program (6 p.m.) that will captivate listeners with a sampling of matchless foot-stomping melodies from around the globe. Emphasis will be on synergistic compositions. The initial show will feature Claude Debussy's nontraditional tonalities combined with Catskill coyote howls and Bulgarian throat singing.

Rumors from Roxbury and Big Indian

In the Catskills, rumors travel faster than the East Branch in a spring thaw. This reporter has been able to put to rest two tales that have buzzed about the mountains this week.

Uber is NOT entering the Roxbury market. Initially it appeared that the lack of taxi service and the need to drive people home from local bars would result in a profitable business for Uber drivers, but the lack of cellular phone service negated such an enterprise.

Jean-Georges Vongerichten is NOT opening an Indian restaurant in Big Indian to compete with the highly successful Peekamoose restaurant. The Jean-George in question is French-Canadian and is NOT the famous restauranteur. Our Jean-George is considering a Native American (Indian) fry bread concession at the next Powwow in Big Indian. Neither Jean-George would return our calls asking for comment.

18. PEPACTON "FLASH OF GREEN" CAPTIVATES CATSKILLS RESIDENTS, THWARTS MARRIAGE PROPOSAL

Atlantic mariners have seen it as have Caribbean cruise ship passengers and tourists packed into Mallory Square in Key West. Last week the flash of green made famous by author John D. MacDonald in his 1962 detective novel of the same name came to the Catskills. Rarely has such a sighting aroused such fervor.

Green flashes are an optical phenomenon that occurs when the rim of the rising or setting sun is just above the horizon. The atmosphere, acting as a prism, refracts the light as a green flash. Green is the first (at sunrise) or last (at sunset) color visible before the sun drops below the horizon.

The Delaware County green flash was observed last Friday evening by Nathan Rigg who was fishing on Pepacton Reservoir with his wife, Cornelia. The North Jersey couple was more interested in enjoying the scenery than doing any serious fishing when Cornelia hooked a small brown trout. She reeled it in and before releasing it, told Nathan to take a picture.

Nathan took out his iPhone 6 and took a forty-two-second long video of Cornelia, the fish, and the setting sun just as it dropped below the treetops at the west end of the reservoir toward Downsville. That is when he saw the vivid green flash. Cornelia did not believe him, but he played her the video.

On the way back to North Jersey, the couple stopped at a bar in Long Eddy where they showed the video to the bartender. The bartender, who holds a doctoral degree in English literature from the State University of New York at Binghamton, was not impressed, but he helped the couple post the video on YouTube.

By morning the video had gone viral with thousands of views and re-postings. Saturday evening brought nearly one hundred people to the reservoir's shores hoping to see the flash. On Sunday there was more than twice that many.

Several people carried signs announcing the "THE RAPTURE IS UPON US." Another read "GOD IS GREEN: SAVE THE ENVIRONMENT." There also were several "GO JETS" and one "VEGANS RULE." Just as the sun set, the crowd spontaneously broke into the song Green, Green made famous by the New Christy Minstrels in 1963. No one saw the flash of green.

Authorities from the New York City Department of Environmental Protection grew alarmed at the size of the crowd and the amount of trash being tossed into the reservoir and along its banks. A number of people also were using the reservoir as a toilet.

Two NYC-DEP policemen downloaded the video, consulted a map, and on Monday went to search the area at the south end of the reservoir. They thought it likely the green flash was from an illicit methamphetamine laboratory explosion.

Following tire tracks up a muddy road, they found what they initially thought was the site of a satanic ritual: a chair with tall poles to which was attached a huge, shattered Becks Beer neon sign. The electric cord was attached to a gasoline generator. Examination revealed the cord was plugged into the 220-240-volt socket of the generator. Near the chair they found a small box containing a ring. On the bottom was the name and address of a jeweler in Margaretville.

When asked if he remembered selling the ring, the jeweler said, "Of course." It was a fake diamond that he sold two weeks earlier for $59.95 plus sales tax. The buyer was a young man who made pizzas at the place across the street.

Even before they were all the way in the door, the young man burst into tears, saying he was sorry and blurting out the story. He had set the whole thing up as a surprise to propose to his girlfriend who loved Beck's beer. The generator came from the Lowes in Oneonta and the Beck's sign from a secondhand store in East Durham. He had no idea the generator produced 220 volts.

He had driven the young woman to the site blindfolded, sat her in the chair, plugged in the sign, and hit the switch. The sign, which operated only on 110 volts, burst in a giant green explosion and his prospective bride fell out of the chair. She had not talked to him since.

On Monday night, the number of people at the reservoir was less than one hundred, many of whom came to see what by then was rumored to be a UFO crash site with dead Martians. There were no green men and no green flash. The crowd drank beer and sang the 1969 Credence Clearwater Revival hit, Green River.

19. TRANSPORTATION DOMINATES LOCAL NEWS THIS WEEK

In an imbroglio eerily reminiscent of the April 2017 United Airlines incident in which a passenger was forcibly dragged off an over-booked flight, a couple from Slovakia who were traveling on a bus from Kingston to Oneonta were similarly removed from their passenger seats. The bus company has since issued a formal apology.

The couple, who spoke no English, had landed at JFK airport that day and were trying to get to Albany where their daughter was a college student. They disembarked from their bus at the station in Kingston to use the facilities. They then re-boarded the wrong bus.

A well-meaning ticket agent noted the error and tried to flag down the bus driver. Failing that, he jumped in his car and set out to catch the bus that was heading west on Washington Avenue at a high rate of speed. A mile past the traffic circle at Route 28, he signaled the bus to pull over.

Not understanding a word said by the agent, the couple tried to prevent being led off the bus. An 84-year old woman passenger headed to Andes began to beat the clerk with an umbrella. Later it was determined the umbrella read "McGovern-Shriver 1972."

A man seated across the aisle who was drinking from a bottle in a brown paper bag began yelling "Terrorists! Terrorists!"

Other passengers jumped on the agent, the umbrella woman, and the drunk man. A young woman on the way to Delhi who filmed everything on a smart phone told this reporter "All hell broke loose. It was awesome!"

Nearly four hours went by before an interpreter could be found and the situation sorted out. Several passengers received medical care. The bus returned to Kingston.

Another Low-Fare Local Option to Europe

Competition between airlines and the use of local airports for international air travel continue to benefit Catskill residents. A new airline—TransMountain Air—last week announced a low-budget flight between the Stanton airport in New Paltz and Broadford Aerodrome on the Isle of Skye in Scotland. The airline has promised to beat the introductory $49 fares offered by Norwegian Air, which two years ago initiated nonstop flights from Newburgh's Steward International Airport to Dublin, Shannon, Edinburgh, Belfast, and Bergen.

TransMountain's 18-passenger single engine jets will fly once a day and all fares will be $48.99. Flights will stop to refuel at Bar Harbor, Maine; Charlottetown on Prince Edward Island; Gander in Newfoundland; and Narsarsuaq Airport in southern Greenland before landing on the Isle of Skye in the mountainous Inner Hebrides Islands.

One cannot exactly pop over to Scotland for dinner, since the five legs of the journey are 346 miles, 730 miles, 917 miles, 773 miles, and 717 miles. TransMountain's planes are certified for a maximum distance of 1050 miles, which gives an added sense of adventure to the Gander to Greenland leg.

This reporter was invited to fly on the inaugural flight last week. [In the interest of full disclosure, I was given the $49 airfare gratis. I did expend another $317 to check a bag, buy water and Doritos (twice), rent a pillow and seat belt, and use the plane's bathroom (three times).]

After landing, rather than enjoy the nineteen-hour return trip, I flew to London and took a plane back to JFK. I will be taking out a home equity loan to pay off my credit card.

In this reporter's opinion, TransMountain Air will most likely appeal to intrepid backpackers with a lot of time on their hands. To save money, consider wearing most of your clothes in layers and sticking everything else in your pockets. Do not check luggage—it is expensive. Carry-ons are not permitted, nor can passengers bring food and beverages aboard.

Because the seats are quite small, I would not recommend the flight for anyone over five-and-a-half feet tall and weighing more than ninety-nine pounds.

20. SCIENCE NEWS IN THE CATSKILLS, OZONE HOLE APPEARS OVER HALCOTTSVILLE

Local Residents See Upside

A spokesperson for the National Aeronautics and Space Administration (NASA) admitted late last week that a hole has appeared in the ozone layer almost directly over Halcottsville in the Catskill Mountains. Such an occurrence is unprecedented. The Halcottsville disconformity is in addition to the much larger hole over Antarctica.

Fearing a panic among residents of Halcottsville, NASA tried to keep the hole a secret, but was forced by an astute Margaretville attorney to make an announcement. The barrister, noticing that Halcottsville residents had great suntans, asked them if they had spent the winter in Florida. None had—instead all lamented they had spent the winter months in Halcottsville shoveling snow.

The attorney, recognizing that something out of the ordinary was occurring, called a friend at Pennsylvania State University's School of Meteorology. The Penn State scientist agreed the situation was an anomaly, so he traveled to the Catskills and sent up weather balloons with sensors that verified the existence of an ozone hole above Halcottsville. NASA was forced to go public.

A team from the Center for Disease Control in Atlanta arrived in Halcottsville this past Monday to tell local residents what they might expect from the increased high-energy ultraviolet-B radiation. Such radiation is normally blocked by the atmospheric ozone layer. Because exposure to UVB rays can damage genetic material in cells, the CDC warned residents to stay inside and, if going out, to slather on a tanning lotion of at least SPF 50 or higher.

At a town-wide meeting, CDC experts repeatedly emphasized that residents should not be alarmed. The hole was likely to close in a matter of months or in a few years at most. Residents who attended the meeting seemed little concerned. Nearly half actually left early when they learned that an ozone layer had nothing to do with hens and eggs.

Far from panicking, Halcottsville has decided to embrace its new status as Sunshine City. A beach and outdoor cafe are slated to be constructed next to Old River Road along Lake Wawaka.

Wawaka Beach is expected to draw huge crowds. Kiosks selling suntan lotion, T-shirts, sunglasses, and Piña Coladas are planned.

A local relator who is a major proponent of the beach is hoping that Halcottsville will become a mecca for college spring breakers and recently married couples. "Who wouldn't want to spend their spring vacation or honeymoon in Halcottsville?"

Scientists Flocking to Catskills, Neanderthal Descendants Plentiful in Local Population

This week the personal DNA testing service 23andMe released their first country-wide maps showing distributions of gene pools. The online maps can be searched for ancestral origins of clusters of individuals living in specific geographical localities across the United States.

For the Catskills the results, none of which provide names or addresses of specific people, are extraordinary. The maps indicate that the 23andMe participants with the highest percentage of Homo neanderthalensis genes in the entire United States are in western Greene, northwestern Ulster, and northern Delaware counties.

Scientists estimate that the modern United States population shares between one to four percent of their genetic makeup with ancient Neanderthals. The Catskill data range is 3 to 8 percent.

The National Institute of Health has sent a team of scientists, including medical staff and anthropologists, to the Catskills hoping to understand why the anomalous distribution exists.

The research team will set up laboratories in key towns to collect gene-rich spit from a large sample of residents to supplement the data gathered from 23andMe participants. Labs will function from 7-9 a.m. in Margaretville, Roxbury, Big Indian, Shandaken, and Wyndham. The early hours for saliva collection are intended to prevent degradation of genes in spit by alcohol that might enter the systems of residents later in the morning.

Anthropologists will be engaging in participant observation among local people in those same towns from 4 to 6 p.m. The assumption is residents are more likely to talk during those hours.

Why the high occurrence of Neanderthal genes in the Catskills exists is unknown. Dr. Rafael Solecki who leads the NIH teams declined to speculate.

When results are interpreted by the team of scientists, the *Catskill Tribune* staff will inform our readers.

21. NEW HAND DRYER FASCINATES ROXBURY DINERS

Who would have thought that a newly installed sanitary device would create such controversy? A local eatery recently replaced their old paper towel dispenser in the bathroom with a brand new, high tech Dyson AirBlade. Popular in New York City movie theater restrooms, the AirBlade produces two streams of heated air that dry wet hands when patrons insert both open hands (with palms toward the front) into slots in the device. Moving hands up and down in the slots allows jets of hot air to do their job.

The effectiveness of the AirBlade has been questioned in several observational studies carried out in men's rooms across the country. Those analyses suggest that ninety-two percent of adult male users of the AirBlade wipe their hands on their pants after using the machines.

It was not the efficiency of the AirBlade that created a hullaba-loo in the small town of Roxbury on the first night the AirBlade was functioning. Rather, according to the restaurant's attorney, it was "the novelty of the dryer" and the fact that "many people were unfamiliar" with its operation. "At least one of the lawsuits filed against the restaurant," according to the attorney, is "the direct result of AirBlade abuse." She added, "Also, my clients—the owners of the restaurant, as well as the building's owners—are in no way responsible for any marital distress precipitated by misuse of the AirBlade. We believe that particular lawsuit is frivolous."

A waitperson at the restaurant, who wanted to remain anonymous, agreed to be interviewed about the night in question: "The AirBlade was working perfectly. Everybody at the bar, our regular crowd, was talking about how neat the dryer was and how it showed that Roxbury was becoming a sophisticated tourist destination with a thriving night life. The problem was we were featuring a two-for-one cocktail night.

"The first incident was about six o'clock. A newly married couple from Atlanta who were honeymooning in the Catskills each had four Cosmos before the woman went into the bathroom. When she didn't come out after about fifteen minutes, the husband got worried and went to look for her. He found her in the bathroom astride the AirBlade, enjoying the hot air.

"Really bad words were exchanged. Among other things, she was yelling that the guy was a loser in bed and she should have married R2 D2, the droid from Star Wars. They guy called her a slut and screamed that he knew something was wrong when she insisted on an American Fellowship Church Life minister instead of a Baptist preacher. She left, apparently grabbed her stuff from their hotel room, and headed for parts unknown in their car. The alienation of affection suit was filed by the guy's brother, an attorney in Druid Hills in Atlanta.

"About 7:15 the same evening, one of the regulars found the new AirBlade in the bath room and apparently decided if he could only get his head in it, the warm air would sober him up so he could go home and face the music. No way his head was going to fit into the slots. He tried and tried to no avail. Finally, he lodged his head between the AirBlade and the wall and pretty much passed out.

"His buddies found him and tried to pull him out, doing some serious damage to his left ear and partially scalping him on the same side. Someone had the good sense to call the Fire Department who came, got him out, and transported him to the Margaretville hospital."

Following these two unfortunate incidents, the restaurant's management team has hired a bathroom attendant to help patrons with the AirBlade and monitor its use. The attendant will be accepting tips.

22. HALLOWEEN HIGH JINKS AND HIGH BEAMS CREATE CONFRONTATION

Repercussions from Halloween continue to reverberate through the Catskill Mountains. The following incident only recently came to light.

About 4 a.m. Wednesday morning following Halloween, two male revelers from a Margaretville costume party decided it was time to walk home down Main Street. One of the two had attended the party dressed as Jesus, while the other was in costume as Mahatma Gandhi, complete with staff and loin cloth.

When Jesus and Gandhi walked in front of the NBT Bank parking lot, the bright lights from a car coming toward them temporarily blinded both men. In retaliation Jesus made a rude hand gesture and Gandhi, a philosophy major in college who believed in nonviolent but positive action, dropped his loin cloth and mooned the three people in the Hyundai.

The three, two women and one man, all of whom were dressed as members of the heavy metal rock band KISS, were returning to Grand Gorge from a Halloween party in Andes. The driver hit the brakes and the three piled out of the car to confront Jesus and Gandhi. Jesus exacerbated the encounter when he snidely enquired, "Who are you supposed to be? Peter, Paul, and Mary?" The KISS trio, who had spent the better part of a week working on their costumes and all day putting on makeup, were incensed.

One of the KISS women then called Gandhi, "Baby Huey," a dia-pered cartoon character from the 1950s. Just as it appeared the five were going to engage in fisticuffs, a New York State Trooper in a patrol car happened by, shining high beams on the group. Not real-izing it was a law officer in the car, all five of the party goers made rude gestures.

Exactly what happened next is a bit uncertain. What is known from a tape provided by law enforcement is that the highway pa-trolman called on his radio for backup, telling the dispatcher, "I've got Jesus and Gandhi and three members of a satanic cult—I need help." The dispatcher responded, "Good luck with that. I'm here with Zsa Zsa Gabor, Joan Rivers, and the Three Bears—everyone else is asleep." The patrolman then exited his car carrying a heavy flashlight and reaching for his holster. About that moment one of the KISS trio began to projectile vomit, hitting Jesus, the patrol-man, and the patrol car, the door of which was open. Chaos ensued.

The patrolman tried to pull his revolver, but it was too slippery to hold. Both it and the flashlight dropped to the ground. Gandhi gingerly picked up the two items and tried to hand them to the officer, but the latter ran into his patrol car and locked the doors, pleading on the radio for backup.

By the time a second patrolman arrived at the scene nearly an hour later, the KISS trio had loaded up Jesus and Gandhi and all five had driven off, but not before Jesus was forced to discard the soiled bed sheet he had been wearing.

The backup patrolman took the first officer, his car, and the flashlight and revolver to the car wash on Fair Street and helped clean everything. The identities of Jesus, Gandhi, and the KISS band members remain unknown to authorities.

23. IS GOD MESSAGING MEEKER HOLLOW RESIDENTS?

Papal Officials Intrigued

A representative from the Roman Curia in the Vatican briefly visited Roxbury to look into two recent incidents that some local people are calling signs from God. Father Guido Sarducci, the Vatican delegate, declined to comment on what he had discovered.

The first incident took place last Friday at a Meeker Hollow farm. A Holstein-Friesian calf born several hours after midnight displayed odd black and white markings on her right side. Once the calf dried, it took only a second for the farmer caring for her to realize that the design resembled the Virgin Mary.

A quick online search confirmed the observation: on the side of the calf was an apparition of the Virgin Mary very similar to that of Our Lady of Fatima who had first revealed herself in 1917 to three shepherd children in a pasture in Fátima, Portugal.

The calf and her mother have been moved to an unspecified pasture, where they will not be bothered by pilgrims eager to see the image.

This reporter visited the farm where the calf was born and spoke with a farmhand. When asked if there were any special plans in store for the calf, a farmhand, apparently unaware of the possible miracle, replied, "Special plans? You mean like a marinade?"

The second Meeker Hollow incident occurred on the same day the calf was born. John Islington was driving his 1987 Ford F-150 XLT pickup truck down Lower Meeker Hollow Road toward the intersection with West Settlement Road when he drifted too far right and clipped a mail box mounted on a concrete post.

Stopping to see what damage he may have caused to the passenger side of his truck Mr. Islington was taken aback by the pattern of dents, rust, and scraped paint on the passenger-side door. Before him was an image of the Virgin Mary.

The woman whose mailbox was run into came out to survey the scene and was just telling Mr. Islington she would take $25 cash to pay for a new box when she noticed the truck door and exclaimed, "My God, man, it's a miracle!"

Mr. Islington decided that $23, all the money he had with him, was a good price for a miracle and paid the woman.

Mr. Islington has parked the truck in front of his house and put up a hand-lettered sign: "$1 To See A Miracle." Thus far there have been few takers.

The possible significance of the calf and the pickup truck has local residents talking. Were the images signs from the heavens? Would there be more apparitions? What was the message being sent?

When asked what she thought that message might be, a longtime resident of Upper Meeker Hollow Road opined, "Perhaps Our Lady of Meeker Hollow is telling us to drink more milk and not text when we drive."

A year has passed and both Vatican authorities and local residents have lost interest in the apparitions about as fast as Moses parted the Red Sea in the 1956 epic movie, The Ten Commandments. The calf was sold to a dairy where she is growing up. Attempts by the owner to pass off milk claimed to have come from the heifer as "Mary's Holy Milk" were not wholly successful. Locals are well aware the adolescent cow is too young to be milked and the Holy Milk is a scam. Tourists, however, have purchased several of the pint bottles.

The markings on the heifer's side have changed as she has grown. Her present owners are divided as to whether the markings now depict Frank Sinatra or Frank Zappa.

Mr. Islington likewise had little success in drawing paying visitors to see his truck door. When a visitor from the Ark Encounter theme park near Lexington, Kentucky, showed up and offered him $100 and two free tickets to tour the ark in exchange for the door, he accepted. Two weeks later he sold the one-door truck to his neighbor for $600. He has retired and is enjoying his windfall. The two tickets are for sale for $20 each.

24. WEDDING BUSINESS CONTINUES TO EXPAND IN THE "MOUNTAINS OF LOVE"

The last decade has witnessed an unprecedented surge in the choice of the Catskills as a venue for weddings. Couples are flocking to the region to tie the knot. It seems everyone loves the natural beauty of the mountains.

Each wedding has an economic impact. Facilities are rented, relatives and wedding guests are housed, caterers engaged, and limousine drivers contracted. Hair stylists, florists, photographers, caterers, and ceremonial officiants are employed. Details proliferate and money flows.

This growth has drawn the attention of a new addition to the nuptial business, a company that calls itself Weddings 'R' Us.

According to Lisa Anderson, one of the founders, "Weddings 'R' Us offers a one-stop service for your wedding. But we can do much more than simply plan a wedding. We will help you find a spouse, and, should you wish, aid you in planning and living your future life together."

A look at the web page of Weddings 'R' Us left this reporter amazed. Are you looking for your life companion, but need help locating him or her? Not a problem. Weddings 'R' Us offers a dating service that guarantees you will find the right person.

Not wanting to get married, but desperately wanting to get your parents off your back? For a few more dollars, Weddings 'R' Us will provide a suitable spouse-to-be surrogate and fake the whole ceremony.

Too shy to pop the question? Weddings 'R' Us will coach you, write your proposal, and arrange a suitable romantic setting. They will even pick out a ring. Too busy to pop the question? A Romeo or Juliet can record their proposal (or have it recorded for you) and have both the recording and the ring delivered by drone.

No detail is too small for Weddings 'R' Us, whether a boutonniere for the best man or a memorable bachelorette party in the town of Shandaken.

Offered also are post-wedding amenities and opportunities. Need a honeymoon planned? Not a problem. How about family planning? Weddings 'R' Us can do that as well.

Company counselors will help you find a place to live, select a name for your baby, decorate the young scion's nursery, and even organize your closets. Weddings 'R' Us also provides its clients with a mobile phone app, putting customers in instant communication with company representatives. The app is available both for iPhones and Android phones.

According to Ms. Anderson, there is not a thing Weddings 'R' Us cannot do to help anyone live a life of fulfillment, the life you've always wanted with the person of your dreams.

Weddings 'R' Us takes VISA and Master Card, but not American Express. If you buy the Whole Life package but are divorced within twelve months of the wedding ceremony you can apply for a ten percent rebate.

25. MISGUIDED PROTEST NEAR HISTORIC TOWN OF BREAKABEEN FIZZLES FAST

A new roadside restaurant on Route 30 between North Blenheim and Breakabeen in Schoharie County was the scene of an abortive protest by an anti-immigrant group based near Oneonta. The group is believed to be associated with the alt-right Reclaim the Catskills movement.

The small restaurant that was the focus of the protest had planned to open next week. Last Saturday a beat-up Honda carrying five protesters parked in front of the eatery. The five got out of the van and began to march around carrying placards.

The protestors were drawn by the words on the restaurant's sign on the front of the building and the sample menu printed beneath:

WE SERVE THE WORLD—
EVERYONE IS WELCOME
Cubans
Plantains
Vietnamese Pho
Samosas

One poster carried by a protestor read "Send Cubans Back to South America;" a second was hand-lettered, "We Speek English Here;" a third announced, "No Foreigners in New York State;" and the fourth, "Pho Go back to NAM." Apparently, the protestors thought the restaurant was a community center for immigrants.

After an hour and a half in the hot sun, the exhausted protesters sat down in front of the restaurant. That is where they were when the young couple who owned the restaurant drove up.

The two patiently explained what their business was and brought out cold drinks for the protestors. One of the protestors had been wearing a rubber Donald Trump mask complete with orange hair and was close to suffering heat stroke.

Somewhat embarrassed, the five protestors got back into their car only to discover that it would not start. The restaurant owners loaded the five into the back of their pickup truck and drove them back to the Oneonta suburbs, towing the broken-down car behind.

26. NEWS BRIEFS: ROXBURY IN DARKNESS ONCE AGAIN

New York Electricity and Gas (NYSEG) officials announced they have traced the cause of the electric outage that left nearly 830 Roxbury households and businesses without power for four-and-a-half hours beginning at 4 a.m. Saturday, June 24.

The malfunction resulted in dairy farmers having to milk their cows by hand and early risers to forgo their morning coffee. No electricity also meant that local residents who had set their alarms for 6:30 a.m. and the Prancing with Paddy local radio show were denied an opportunity to practice Irish dancing.

NYSEG said that a main distribution line transformer blew up.

The accident was caused by human error. Three couples from Brooklyn staying in a weekend rental just off Route 30 near the outskirts of Grand Gorge all had turned on their high wattage Dyson Supersonic hair dryers at approximately the same moment.

The six hipsters had arisen early and were styling their hair prior to a dawn hike and body toxin cleansing ritual led by a local guru.

In addition, three DeLonghi ESAM6620 Gran Dama Super Automatic Beverage Centers the visitors had brought with them all turned on precisely at 4 a.m. The electric grid could not take the sudden power needed to run the nine high wattage appliances.

Movie to Be Shot Locally, Extras Needed

An Emmy award-winning producer, who maintains a weekend home in Woodstock, is scouting locations in and around town for a feature-length film entitle, The Pollinator.

In an interview with our entertainment reporter the director revealed, "For many years I have been fascinated with two movies: The Terminator and Ulee's Gold. Bees, like androids, have power. Bees also are crucial for life as we know it. What would happened if the apiary community turned on us, rebelling again our use of pesticides and our mowing meadows?"

Though the producer declined to reveal too much about the script, he did say that pterodactyl-size giant metallic transformer killer bees with faces like Arnold Schwarzenegger would play major roles in the film. He also stated it was his intent to hire a number of local beekeepers as extras, noting, "Generally they aren't afraid to be stung." He declined to be more specific, though he did add: "And I am looking for investors. Here is a chance to be part of Hollywood history."

The movie's graphic pollination scenes are expected to draw an "R" rating from the Motion Picture Association of America.

Loch Ness Monster in Pepacton Reservoir? Locals Claim They Have Photos

Two women who were fishing from the south shore of Pepacton Reservoir last week claim to have seen a Loch Ness-like sea serpent swimming in the reservoir. They told local authorities the monster was in the same place two days in row, both times about 5 a.m. The two refused to show iPhone photos they had taken, stating they were negotiating to sell the images to the National Enquirer.

An early morning hiker on the north shore on one of the same days reported he saw what looked like a scuba diver in a small boat with some sort of a platform on the stern. *Catskill Tribune* reporters are presently researching both sightings. Are the two related? We think so. Look for an in-depth *Catskill Tribune* article in the next few weeks.

Karaoke Promises to Revive Night Life

A Roxbury bar and restaurant plans to make an announcement soon naming Tuesday nights, "Katskill Karaoke Knight." Instead of the usual songs, contestants will accompany New Age spa music with bird calls and other vocalizations.

According to the owner, "We have some world-class turkey callers out there, along with other talented people who can mimic coyotes, owls, fawns, howler monkeys, those funny noises when you get a text on iPhone, and the Roxbury fire station's noon siren. Roxbury is going to be the area's late-night place to be on Tuesdays, 6:45 to 7:30 p.m."

CATSKILL TRIBUNE—Your Favorite Source of Alternative News in the Mountains—To Expand

Acceding to public demand, the publisher of the *Catskill Tribune* announced yesterday at a cocktail hour staff meeting that two new features would appear occasionally in the newspaper.

Our nature editor is taking on a "police beat-like" column tentatively called "Constable's Corner," where one can read about the illegal things their neighbors have been up to.

The social editor has been assigned a column titled "Life and Love in the Catskills." As presently envisioned the column will answer reader queries about finding happiness in the Catskills not related to food, drinking, cats and other pets, homeless animals, vacation trips, or politics (in other words, not anything you are likely to see on Facebook).

27. CONSTABLE'S CORNER— CRIME IN THE CATSKILLS

The *Catskill Tribune* is pleased to publish our first "Constable's Corner" column. Today we focus on two untoward incidents, both of which occurred last week.

The first was in Grand Gorge not far off Route 23 on the way to Prattsville. Two neighbors who have lived next to one another for more than thirty years had a falling out that required intervention by law enforcement and fire department officials.

Ronald Holden and Robert Freeman and their spouses occupy adjoining houses that share a single well. The houses were built about 1946 by two brothers who thought it would be less expensive that way. Subsequent deeds all spell out the arrangement.

Up until last week Holden and Freeman and their families had for the most part gotten along very well and there were no disagreements about water usage.

All that began to change in November when the neighbors supported different candidates in the last United States presidential election. Bickering among the two escalated. The situation was aggravated when the well began to take up silt and sometimes ran dry for a day or two.

The rains that have blessed our Roxbury communities over the last two months replenished the well's water, but did little to cool the antagonism between the two husbands.

Last week Freeman hooked up a sprinkler next to four Crispin apple trees. Holden watched the water run for more than twelve hours and then could stand it no longer. At 11 p.m., while everyone else in both houses was asleep, he entered Freeman's yard, turned off the water, and then used a hatchet to cut the hose into more than two hundred pieces. He was in the midst of sawing down the second apple tree when Freeman came outside to see what the noise was.

The two men exchanged words, with Freeman calling Holden a Trump-loving Soviet Nazi and Holden retorting that Freeman was too stupid to know that the Soviet Union no longer existed and that Nazis were from Germany. At that point the two men were separated by their spouses.

Freeman stewed about the incident for two days. About 4 a.m. on the second night, he snuck into Holden's yard, turned on a hose, and put the end through the partially open window of Holden's restored 1949 F-1 half-ton Ford pickup truck, his pride and joy.

The next morning the men accosted one another with hunting rifles. One spouse called the police, while the other phoned the Grand Gorge fire department.

A policeman arrived along with the assistant fire chief and together they calmed both men. The two neighbors have agreed to meet separately with an anger management counselor. Mr. Holden's spouse noted, "None of this would have happened if the T-Bar hadn't closed. We went there as a foursome every week. Now we just sit home and watch all that crap on TV."

The second incident took place on Saturday night in Roxbury after a seventy-six-year old grandmother living on Upper Meeker Hollow Road decided it was time to smoke marijuana for the first time in her life.

The previous week her grandson had given the woman a small bag of locally grown cannabis and showed her how to smoke it in an old corn cob pipe. She put the bag on her mantle and looked at it all week.

Following one Makers Mark before dinner and another while she was watching Seinfeld reruns on television, she decided it was time. She apparently smoked much of the bag.

At that point it seemed to the grandmother it would be great fun driving her old tractor into downtown Roxbury to look for friends. She hopped on, fired it up, and headed east down Upper Meeker Hollow Road and then north on Stratton Falls Road. Along the way she sang, "I've fallen and I can't get up" at the top of her lungs.

As she drove by the old Brookdale creamery just before the railroad crossing, a police car passed her in the opposite direction. Realizing something was amiss, the law officer did a power slide and reversed direction, turned on lights and siren, and went in pursuit.

The tractor driver was having none of it. She continued down the road.

The police car drove ahead of her, crossed the tracks, and did a half turn blocking the road. The grandmother did not miss a beat. She jogged left and headed up the railroad tracks. The policeman chased after her on foot.

About a half mile north of the crossing the vibration caused the tractor driver's lower dentures to dislodge. She began to sing, "My teeth have fallen and they can't get up either." At that point the exhausted policeman walked back to his car and called in a report on his radio. At least one person monitoring a police scanner heard the conversation and the incident was the talk of Roxbury the next day.

Meanwhile the tractor bounced past the old Roxbury train depot and turned left up the road to the Shepherd Hills golf course. Near the golf green on the left just before the club house, the grandmother drove into the woods, turned off the ignition, and went to sleep on the edge of the green. Employees found her next morning, still asleep.

Once authorities identified the grandmother, they visited her at home. She agreed to give up driving the tractor and to receive counseling from an American Fellowship Church minister she had met at a wedding. Her concerned neighbors traced her journey down the tracks and found her dentures, which miraculously were not broken. Since no harm was done, the case is considered closed.

A year later we checked in with the Meeker Hollow resident. We learned the incident was a wake-up call for the grandmother. No more sitting around the house watching the QVC shopping network and Seinfeld all day and night. She took driving lessons, got her license, and bought a used car that she uses to visit restaurants, bars, and shops from Oneonta to Woodstock.

Her grandson, feeling badly about the tractor incident, helped his grandmother pick out a Lenova laptop computer (on QVC) and get it hooked up to MTC internet. He then spent hours with her showing her how to surf the net, opening a new world. Grandma became quite proficient.

Eventually the Upper Meeker Hollow Road senior citizen found her way to J-Date and began exchanging emails with a widower in Bronxville, New York. When asked why she used a Jewish dating site she admitted she always liked "those circumcised guys." She added that the FarmersOnly.com dating site had produced, in her words, a lot of "men who thought a good time was planting garlic and driving over to Phoenicia."

She and her Bronxville beau have become a couple and are splitting time between their respective homes. Though most of her family is scandalized, the grandson told us his Nana is "the coolest" around.

28. LIFE AND LOVE IN THE CATSKILLS

The *Catskill Tribune* is pleased to present our very first "Life and Love in the Catskills" column. We were astounded at the number of letters submitted. Here is a small selection.

TO THE LIFE AND LOVE EDITOR: You're not going to have much to write about, because there is not a lot of either life or love in the Catskills. (Signed) Lonely, Broke, Depressed, and Hating Everything Irish Here in East Durham

DEAR LONELY, BROKE, DEPRESSED, ETC.: Au contraire. The hills are alive with music and Catskillians are filled with happiness and good will towards their fellow beings (especially if that being is a cat or a dog; humans? not so much). My advice for meeting people is to join a book club at the local library. (One would assume there is a library in East Durham and one might also assume that you read.) Then gather up all the aluminum cans you can find and cash them in at the local market. You can make a few dollars a day. Most importantly, quit watching the news on television; not knowing what is going on in our government might cheer you up. And lastly, ignore all that Irish stuff in East Durham. Instead join the local chapter of Goths-R-Us. They meet each full moon in the bar just down the road in Freehold. The group often holds joint meetings with the Anarchists-R-Us Club. You will have a blast and your spirits will certainly be altered. Good luck. Remember, happiness is all around you.

DEAR LIFE AND LOVE EDITOR: When I graduated from high school, I enlisted for a two-year hitch in the United States Coast Guard. The recruiter promised that I would be assigned to the east coast of New England, so I would be near home and Janie, my high school steady. When I signed up, Janie promised to wait for me forever. But the recruiter lied to me and I was stationed near Nome, Alaska. After twenty months I saved enough money to come back home to the Catskills on leave. I planned to propose to Janie. But when I went by her parents' house, they told me she was married, had a kid with another on the way, and had moved to Florida. She lied to me, too. What should I do? (Signed) Jilted, Cold, and Disillusioned

DEAR JILTED, ETC., ETC.: Re-up for another two years and hope for a warmer posting.

DEAR LIFE AND LOVE EDITOR: I am totally in love with my awesome history teacher who looks like Madonna used to look. I think she might like me, too. She asked to see me after class. She was looking right into my eyes when she said, "Other than the two paragraphs you copied from Wikipedia, your essay on Thomas Edison's invention of the light bulb was possibly the worst thing I have read in twelve years of teaching." How can I tell her it is OK to let me know how she really feels about me? (Signed) C Student in Boiceville (OK, my average is actually a D plus).

DEAR D+ STUDENT, ETC. ETC.: If I were you, I would drop history and take chemistry. I can almost guarantee you will not like your chemistry teacher.

DEAR LIFE AND LOVE EDITOR: I am being held at an assisted living facility run by Riverside Federated USA. We 'inmates' call it RFU, as in our "Relatives F-----d Us." Everyone here who can still think hates the place.

A group of us women who still have their wits are looking for some action. The male inmates here aren't worth a toot. Most have loose parts, if you know what I mean.

We invited over the local Rotary Club and then the Elks Club and they were a bunch of losers. We next organized date nights in the cafeteria, thinking a romantic atmosphere might help.

My first date seemed all right for about three minutes. Then I realized he thought I was President Eisenhower. I told him I had to go to the bathroom to find Mamie and never went back to the table. On the second date night my dining companion fell asleep before the entrée arrived and then peed all over himself.

We have raised nearly $5000 bucks. Can you arrange to have the Chippendales visit for an evening? If you can't, our second choice is a motorcycle gang. (Signed) Hot and horny, but not in hospice.

DEAR HOT, ETC.: I know the feeling and I sympathize with you. I have contacted the Association of Tele-Evangelists who said they can take care of your needs and that $5000 as well. They will be in touch.

29. GANGSTER'S TREASURE LOST IN CATSKILLS

Part 1 of the Dutch Schultz Saga

For more than eighty years, crime buffs and treasure hunters have looked. But until now no one has had any luck finding where in the Catskills Prohibition-era mobster Dutch Schultz buried his cache of money, jewelry, and guns.

In June a diver from Florida and his brilliant girlfriend found the treasure under the waters of Pepacton Reservoir. They then quickly slipped away to the Caribbean, taking Schultz's loot.

Ask anyone in the Catskills if they know who Arthur Flegenheimer is and you would likely draw a blank stare. Mention Dutch Schultz, however, and nearly everyone can identify him as a New York City gangster of the same ilk as Legs Diamond. Few, however, know that at one time Schultz (who began life as a Flegenheimer) operated stills in and around Phoenicia while running illicit alcohol to New York City. Dutch Schultz and the Catskills share a history together.

Born in New York City in 1902 to Herman and Jennie Flegenheimer, young Arthur entered a life of crime when he was a teenager. At age seventeen he was arrested and jailed. The incarceration did little to curb his appetite for illegal activities, especially bootlegging.

By the time he was in his late twenties, he was known as Dutch Schultz, a major figure in the Big Apple underworld. At one point, J. Edgar Hoover, then head of the FBI, named Dutch Schultz "Public Enemy Number One."

When things got too hot in New York City, Schultz moved to the Catskills to manufacture booze. Schultz likely knew the region from his early boyhood when he went from town to town with a relative of his mother's, a traveling salesman based in eastern Pennsylvania.

Setting up operations in the Catskills did not hide Schultz from rival gangsters nor from Thomas E. Dewey, then a federal prosecutor. Dewey vowed to close down Schultz's operation. Schultz's response was to plan Dewey's assassination. Alarmed at what the government's response to the murder of a federal prosecutor might be, Albert Anastasia, another mobster, ordered a hit on Schultz.

On October 23, 1935, Dutch Schultz was gunned down in the men's room of a restaurant in Newark, along with several of his men. Gravely wounded, Schultz was taken to a Newark hospital, where he died the next night. Before Schultz died, policemen continued to question him, writing down everything he said, whether or not it made sense.

Among his incoherent ramblings was mention of Dutch wanting to be driven back to the Catskills to retrieve government bonds and millions of dollars from a box. Lawmen and gangsters, the latter including both Schultz's associates and his rivals, all believed that Schultz had hidden his wealth prior to carrying out the plan to have Thomas Dewey killed. That plan had been cut short by his untimely visit to a Newark urinal.

Schultz's treasure box was thought to be a safe or suitcase-size, waterproof metal container made specially to hold the loot, estimated at $7 million. The box was buried by Schultz and Bernard

"Lulu" Rosencrantz, his lieutenant who made a map of the location. Unfortunately, Lulu was one of those shot at the same time as Schultz. Lulu lived a day longer than Dutch before also succumbing to bullet wounds.

After Schultz and Rosencrantz died, other members of the gang fell out over ownership of the map, which no one could decipher. No one has ever found the cached treasure, though many have tried.

In 2005 the television show "Unsolved Mysteries" recounted the story of Dutch Schultz's lost loot, unleashing a new generation of treasure seekers.

Two of the people who watched that program were aboard a schooner in the Caribbean. Maxwell (Max) and Constance (Connie) had met in an archaeology class at Florida State University in the mid-1970s. Max was a scuba diver and after graduating with his bachelor's degree went to work for the National Park Service's underwater division. In 1980 he moved to Key West and took a job as a diver with Mel Fisher's Treasure Salvors Company.

Connie left FSU with a BS degree and entered graduate school in California, where she was one of the early adherents of what is now known as Geographic Information System (GIS). She also specialized in the application of remote sensing to finding and interpreting underwater archaeological sites. In 1980 she too moved to Key West to work for Mel Fisher. There she reconnected with Max.

The young couple was in Key West when Treasure Salvors divers found the wreck of the Spanish galleon Santa Margarita that had gone down about 30 miles east of Key West in 1622. They also were there five years later when the Margarita's sister ship, Nuestra Señora de Atocha, was located. Fisher and associates recovered more than forty tons of silver and gold worth $450 million from the vessel.

Many of the Key West divers and support staff drank and smoked away their share of the loot. Connie invested her and Max's portions. In 1986 she heeded the advice of some of her West Coast friends and bought several thousand shares of Apple stock and along with those of other emerging companies. Eleven years later she liquidated a host of equities and took a chance on a new company called Amazon from which she had been ordering books.

Today Max and Connie are very, very rich. The new millennium found them sailing the world on their schooner. They also were getting bored. When they watched the Unsolved Mysteries program, they looked at one another and said, "If anyone can find that treasure, we can."

30. DIVING FOR DOLLARS

Part 2 of the Dutch Schultz Saga

After six months of sleuthing in FBI archives in Washington, DC, Connie turned up what was said to be an exact hand-drawn copy of the original map that Rosencrantz had drafted. The map showed a configuration of what appeared to be the outlines of eleven buildings situated along a street. Behind one building there was an X.

The only thing written on the map were the letters AF print-ed inside the building next to the X. Everyone who had seen the map in the late 1930s assumed that AF was the initials of Arthur Flegenheimer, Dutch Schultz's birth name.

Via Skype this reporter carried out two interviews with Max and Connie (who asked that their last names not be given). They also declined to give their exact location, but it was clear from the image on my computer screen that they were aboard a large sailboat likely anchored off a Caribbean island.

This reporter was able to track the couple by finding names and telephone numbers on papers they had put in their trash at a rent-al house near Andes. Like many visitors to the Catskills, Max and Connie mistakenly thought that once you put the trash bag out the door, it would be picked up and discarded. Instead coyotes or bears strew the trash all through the adjacent woods where I found the papers.

After I contacted them, Max and Connie told me how over nearly a year-and-a-half they compared the Rosencrantz map with maps from the 1930s of Catskill towns. According to Connie, "We started with Phoenicia and then moved on to Big Indian, Boiceville, Pine Hill, Shandaken, Margaretville, and every other town. None of them correlated with the map, so we looked at them all again. It was a laborious process and we nearly gave up.

"Then we had the bright idea to look at the four towns inundated by the creation of Pepacton Reservoir in the 1950s: Arena, Pepacton, Shavertown, and Union Grove. Bingo! Arena was a hit. Max and I both said—a reservoir? That means diving and remote underwater sensing, just our things. It gave us renewed purpose.

"We spent nearly three years gathering data from color infra-red aerial photos and every map, photograph, and description we could find. I felt like I lived in Arena in another life.

"Correlating Lulu's map with Arena's layout indicated that the building behind which Shultz and Rosencrantz buried the box was the Arena firehouse. AF did not stand for 'Arthur Flegenheimer,' it was 'Arena firehouse.' Schultz likely knew Arena from traveling through the East Delaware River region in his boyhood with his mother's relatives.

"Before the reservoir was flooded, the firehouse was removed, along with many other of Arena's buildings and everyone who lived there, dead and alive. But the firehouse's stone foundations were left behind as were those of other buildings

"We spent several more years going over the data and calculating as best we could GPS locations for every corner of Arena's buildings. Then it took nearly another year to plan and buy the equipment we would need. We also had to figure out how to get everything to the Catskills. Fortunately, friends from our Tallahassee days were living in Delaware County and gave us a lot of pointers regarding logistics, while not asking a lot of questions.

"We arranged to have a boat with a dive platform on the stern and an outboard motor towed to a house near Andes we had leased for six months over the internet. As it turned out we could have rented it for only a week.

"A huge metal shipping container of equipment was delivered to the rental house, having been trucked from Tampa. Everything was there when we arrived.

"Our ace in the hole was an Edgetech 6205 Multi Phase Echo Sounder, a state-of-the-art remote sensing device that shows what is below water in beautiful, living color. The images on our computer screens were incredible."

Max then took up the story. "We planned to work in the reservoir each day from first light; in June that's about 4:30 a.m. to sunup, and then again for a couple of hours after sunset before full dark. We hoped not to attract attention.

"But we needed a 'Jedi mind trick' in case anyone saw us and got curious. I thought maybe we could buy a big plastic Loch Ness sea serpent and attach it to our boat. I figured people would ignore us and focus on the monster. We couldn't find anything like that, but when driving through Woodstock on our way to Andes we found a large plastic unicorn float. We bought it and later used our scuba tank compressor to pump it up.

"The boat was so loaded with computers and other equipment I was afraid any waves might swamp us. But there were no problems. Connie's GPS numbers and the Edgetech images were right on the mark. On the second day, I went over the side with my scuba gear and located the firehouse foundation in less than thirty minutes. The water was not that deep and it was an easy dive. By dawn I had attached a small buoy to where the box likely was buried. Silt was not as bad as we had feared.

"That evening we returned and I dug into the bottom and less than three feet down, I found the box and wrapped straps around it. Connie and I pulled it up. It was a pretty exciting moment. Years of research and planning and it took only forty-eight hours to actually put our hands on Dutch Schultz's legendary lost treasure.

"We drove back to the rental house, called someone to pick up the boat and equipment, called the rental agent to say we were leaving, and headed to UPS in Kingston where we shipped the box to ourselves. Then we drove to New York and hopped on a plane. Incredibly we had found Dutch Schultz's legendary treasure."

This reporter asked what was in the box. According to Connie, the money, bonds, and jewels that Schultz was thought to have had were indeed there, along with two solid gold display pistols. Everything was in a large bank safety box that had been put inside a specially made steel box with carefully welded seams. The watertight outer box and contents weighed about twenty pounds.

Max joked that the hardest part of the operation was opening the box.

31. SENTIENT CHIPMUNKS IN CATSKILLS LEAVE ZOOLOGISTS DUMBFOUNDED

Harvard University ethologist Roger Essex-Smith III was visiting friends near Roxbury four years ago when his curiosity was aroused by two chipmunks.

Professor Essex-Smith, a specialist in the behavior of small rodents such as voles and mice, was exiting Roxbury Run onto Scudder Hill Road to have lunch in Roxbury, when he noticed two small bumps on the right side of the road ahead of him. As he got closer, he saw the bumps were chipmunks.

Not wanting to run them over, Professor Essex-Smith slowed a bit. It was a good decision, because at the last second one of the chipmunks darted across the road in front of the car. Thinking the chipmunk might not have made it, the professor looked in his rearview mirror.

Much to his amazement the two chipmunks had met in the middle of the road and appeared to be high-fiving one another. As he reports in an article just published in the Journal of Rodentia, "It was the most incredible thing I have even seen in the animal world. They were playing a game."

The article, co-authored with two graduate students and entitled "Behavior of a Tamias striatus Population in the Catskill Mountains" reports three-and-a-half years of research on chipmunks living in

Roxbury Run in the town of Roxbury. To say that the article has generated controversy in the zoological world would be an understatement. It has literally turned our knowledge of rodents inside out.

In an interview Professor Essex-Smith stated "I was fascinated by the two chipmunks. I spent the next three days in Roxbury Run sitting outside, watching chipmunks and taking notes. At night I searched the internet to read studies of chipmunk behavior. Nothing I found explained what I observed."

Several months later the professor sent a field team to trap chipmunks in Roxbury Run. A second team was sent to another location randomly selected (it turned out to be near Willow, which is west of Woodstock in Ulster County). In each location, twenty live traps were spaced along 200 meters of stone fence.

The baited traps were visited twice daily. Chipmunks that were caught were measured, weighed, sexed, photographed, and the bottom of each right back paw was painted with an indelible dye. At the end of the first week, as reported in the Rodentia journal article, fifty-seven chipmunks were trapped in Willow (seven were caught twice). But in Roxbury Run, the total number of chipmunks was only two!

According to Essex-Smith, "Everyone involved in the research was flabbergasted! We switched traps and teams and did it all again. The results were pretty much the same. The Roxbury Run chipmunks were a lot shrewder than those in Willow. They knew to avoid the traps."

The experiment was repeated several additional times with chipmunk populations in other locations. There was no doubt the Roxbury chipmunks were much smarter than other chipmunks.

How could that be? Had the Roxbury Run chipmunks evolved into a more intelligent population? That seems to be the case.

Securing a grant from the National Science Foundation, the professor took up a year residency in Roxbury Run. The account in Rodentia reporting on his field work is informative.

"I erected a cover over the outdoor patio of the unit I was living in and sat there twelve hours a day observing and taking notes. I also had two cameras set up filming in different directions. At times I could not believe what I was seeing.

"One evening a small bobcat jumped on the stone fence where many of the chipmunks lived and casually walked toward one adult male. At the last second, the bobcat lunged forward intending to grab the chipmunk, but Male 17 (as I had designated him) disappeared into the stones of the fence. At the same moment Female 22 popped up behind the bobcat and started dancing around. The bobcat reversed direction and ran toward her. She disappeared and Male 17 made another appearance, drawing the predator back in his direction. They were harassing the bobcat!

"Once I was bored when not much was happening, so I moved a television onto the patio to watch a soccer match. I regularly snacked on beer nuts, so I usually had a bowl around. The first time I turned on the TV, a chipmunk (Male 11) showed up, ate some nuts, and began watching the soccer match.

"The next day six chipmunks were there. Female 12 quickly learned that by standing on the remote she could change the channel. That usually caused a lot of unhappy chirping among the other chipmunks.

"Because it was a smart TV, I opened Netflix and rented Disney's 1989-1990 TV series Chip 'n Dale: Rescue Rangers. At one point there were twelve chipmunks watching. One high-fived me.

"Over the next few days, Female 12 learned how to turn the TV on and select old Chip 'N Dale episodes. More than once at night I woke up to the sound of the TV and chipmunks chirping."

Professor Essex-Smith recently gave up his tenured faculty position at Harvard University and is now living full time in Roxbury Run.

He intends to study the reason why the local chipmunks have evolved intellectually. "Can it be diet or interaction with the humans living in Roxbury Run or something else? I hope to find out."

When I last spoke with him, the professor opined that his new colleagues were more interesting than some of the people he had left behind in academia. He also cautioned all of us to watch out for chipmunks when driving.

Almost a year after this story first appeared, Professor Essex-Smith still lives in Roxbury Run surrounded by several generations of chipmunks whom he continues to study and socialize with.

In a recent conversation with the *Catskill Tribune*, the professor reported that he may have discovered the reason for the smart chipmunks' intelligence. About six years ago, a retired couple living in Roxbury Run began feeding the chipmunks gummy bears, specifically "Albanese 12 Assorted Flavor Gummi Bears" that the couple ordered in five-pound bags from Amazon, twenty pounds at a time.

Professor Essex-Smith began buying the same gummy bears and has been feeding them to squirrels to see the result. Within months, the local squirrels have taken an interest in television. They and the chipmunks began vying for control of the TV remote. Being larger, the squirrels were not gentle in tuning in old Rocky (the flying squirrel) and Bullwinkle cartoons and movies. To keep peace, the professor was forced to buy a second television and have a second cable box installed. To cover his new expenses, he lamented that he is dipping into his 503(b) retirement account.

Apparently, a large number of the professor's Roxbury Run human neighbors have taken up eating Albanese gummy bears.

32. FAT FREEZING FEATURED AT NEW FACILITY

Christian Potok, a self-proclaimed cowboy from Queens in New York City, has returned to the Catskills with a new entrepreneurial initiative. Readers will remember that Mr. Potok had previously announced he was building a History of Cow Brands Museum in Bovina, along with an on-site oyster bar.

That project fell through when Mr. Potok was unable to garner a license to sell liquor at the oyster bar. According to Mr. Potok, he had some "outstanding issues" related to an unsuccessful roof repair business he owned in Long Island after Hurricane Sandy.

Fat freezing to lose weight is the latest way to rid thighs, upper arms, and stomachs of fat cells. The procedure, often marketed as CoolSculpting, is non-surgical and has brought dermatologists and other medical practitioners new patients and lucrative profits.

According to an article in the New York Times, a medical practice that "averaged two patients a week, with four treatments each" would garner a profit of $200,000 per year.

CoolSculpting works with a suction device that pulls fat cells to the skin surface where they are frozen, a process that kills the cells. Later the body rejects the dead material. The procedure, which requires multiple treatments to show results, has been approved by the Food and Drug Administration.

Mr. Potok agreed to sit down with this reporter and discuss his new business, expected to open in Stamford as soon as the weather turns cold.

According to the charismatic Mr. Potok, "I intend to have a high-end, up-market operation. And it's going to be much more organic and natural then those big city clinics with their huge energy-guzzling machines."

In response to my question about the actual process he intends to use to freeze fat cells, Mr. Potok went into a long explanation. Basically, he plans to use ice cubes that will be placed in old pillow cases and taped onto those parts of the body that patients wish to have treated. A vacuum cleaner is also involved.

"I picked up an industrial-size ice machine from a Holiday Inn Express on Long Island that was flooded out in Sandy." He also acquired a 14.4 cubic feet freezer from a sea food restaurant destroyed in the hurricane. "It was a little funky from the rotted fish, but I've had it and the ice machine in storage for a number of years and it ought to be OK by now." The pillow cases also are from the defunct Holiday Inn Express.

"When the ice cubes melt, we harvest the water and use a pump to put it back into the ice machine. It is a very economical and ecologically closed system … no waste."

Mr. Potok added, "I'm also going to sell ice cream at discount. Some deal, huh? They come in to lose fat and then take a gallon of chocolate ice cream home. Wait, wait, don't print that, OK?"

When asked if he had anything additional he wanted prospective clients to know, he said, "Tell 'em we're going to be showing free movies they can watch while getting their parts frozen. I've got all five of the Ice Age movies on DVD and also that Disney one about Elsa, the Ice Queen. And Wi-Fi will be available for almost nothing."

33. FAT FREEZING FACILITY FAILS AMID LAWSUIT, HEALTH ISSUES

County Health Department Officials have shut down the new fat freezing facility in Stamford after only one day of operation. The owner, Christian Potok, the self-proclaimed cowboy from Queens in New York City, had envisioned a soft opening for Eskimo Heaven, billed as a non-invasive, Inuit-related weight-loss method similar to CoolSculpting.

Soon after 9 a.m. on opening day, several clients were lined up outside Eskimo Heaven, but when blood-curdling screams were heard emanating from the first customer, everyone in the queue quickly departed. That first customer, a man from Hobart, has filed a lawsuit against the business. The gentleman's attorney allowed him to speak with this reporter from his bed in a local medical facility.

According to the Hobart resident, the ice packs applied to his upper arms and thighs brought on hyperthermia. Even worse were the round welts left by the vacuum device used to draw frozen fat cells to the surface of the man's soft tissues.

Speaking in a hoarse whisper, the Hobart resident recounted his experience. "The vacuum hurt like hell and left about twenty-one-and-a-half-inch in diameter marks that look like suction hickeys from an amorous giant octopus' tentacles. Almost as bad was the rotten stench from the ice cubes they tied on me.

"After the treatment, I drove myself back to Hobart to go to work at the bookstore where I am employed. By the time I walked from my parking space to the store, seven cats were following me. My boss took one look at all the round red spots and the cats and fired me before the smell even hit her.

"At that point, I went straight to the hospital and called an attorney, who called authorities. I may be scarred for life."

When Mr. Potok was questioned about the customer's complaints and the arrival of the authorities, he brushed off the incident as "opening day jitters." He did say that he needed to do more cleaning on that old fish freezer in which he stored the ice.

Asked about the pending lawsuit, Mr. Potok seemed nonplussed. "I set this operation up as an LLC. They won't get nothing out of me."

Eskimo Heaven remains closed.

34. CAMPERS ON PERCH LAKE MOUNTAIN VANISH

Join Us in the Stars: Part 1 of a 2-Part Investigation

In mid-August this year, Marvin Rogers, a licensed New York State guide, smelled campfire smoke while leading two out-of-town clients on an early morning hike up Shavertown Trail. The well-marked path ascends Perch Lake Mountain, not far from Pepacton Reservoir in Delaware County.

Seating the two hikers on a log bench next to the lake, Marvin went northwest through the woods towards where he thought the smoke was coming from. Sure enough, about 250 yards off the trail, he came upon four tents arranged in a small circle.

His first impression was that it was the neatest campsite he had ever seen. A longer look made him realize the tents, a small propane cooking stove, a fold-out table with chairs, and even a solar generator all looked new—brand new.

Marvin walked into the camp and called, "Hello, anyone here?" It was a simple query, but one that has led to an extraordinary mystery and, just perhaps, one of the most remarkable events in the history of humankind.

After Marvin returned his two clients to Roxbury, he came back to the Shavertown Trail camp. There, at the request of Ms. Kathy Young, one of the campers, he made himself comfortable. Over the next two hours, he listened to an incredible story.

That evening Marvin called me and we met at the hotel in Andes. We sat outside on the front porch steps under the stars and Marvin told me what Ms. Young had told him; I took notes. Here is her account, presented as a first-person narrative, though it is of course not an actual transcript.

According to Ms. Young:

"I was raised in Cocoa, Florida, near Cape Canaveral, wanting desperately to grow up and be an astronaut. But it didn't happen—I found out I hated heights and puked on Ferris wheels. Second choice was graduate work in astrophysics at Cal Tech. After I got my PhD, I went to work for an engineering firm in Connecticut. I hated the job.

"On a lark I applied for a position as a TV science editor for Fox News in New York City. I got the job, though I soon learned that in reality, I was a glorified news reader. Fox News was a cesspool of sexism, but I couldn't find another job that paid as well.

"On June 15, I glanced at my email on my tablet. The account was one that I use only for family members. I opened an incoming message that had no name or information indicating the sender. It read, 'You have been selected. More information to arrive on June 17.' I noticed two things right off the bat. First was that the time of the text was 6:07 a.m.—by chance, June 7 is my birthday (I love numbers). The other thing was that I could not delete the email, nor could I forward, print, or copy it. Strange. I thought it likely had come from a spammer trying to sell me a timeshare who had figured out a clever way to keep their ad out there. But how did they get my secret email address?

"It sort of crapped me out, so I took the tablet to the tech people at Fox and asked them to fix it. Later a woman called to have me pick it up, confessing she had been unsuccessful in cleaning out the message. The IT woman told me she had never seen anything like it: 'Whoever figured out how to do that is way ahead of what I know.'

"I forgot all about it until Friday morning. The old email was gone, replaced by a new one, again with a time stamp of 6:07 a.m. I read the long email at least a half dozen times, thinking it was a hoax.

"The email said that I and three other people had been selected to be 'transmuted' (I had to look that word up to be certain I understood what it meant) to 'another world' occupied by 'others.' The other world was quite literally in the stars, specifically a super-Earth, exoplanet known as Kepler-62f that orbits a star similar to our own sun in the constellation of Lyra. It was 1,200 light-years from where I was in downtown Manhattan.

"I was asked to be at a specific Global Positioning System (GPS) location on Tuesday, August 15, and to bring camping gear and be prepared to be there for several days. The message indicated the other three people would be there as well.

"Did I think it was all a lot of bunk? You bet. For verification, the email suggested I call my old Cal Tech professor, Jack DeShannon, and ask him if the RATAN-600 (Radio Astronomical Telescope of the Academy of Sciences) telescope at Zelenchukskaya in southwestern Russia had picked up anything odd coming from the constellation Lyra last evening at 6:07 p.m. EST time.

"I called Jack's office and got his secretary. After I identified myself she said, 'I know he is going to want to talk with you.'

"When Jack came on the line he said, 'How did you do it?' 'Do what,' I asked?' 'Send radio waves from Keplar-62F that spelled out 'Kathy Young' in Morse code.' "

35. CAMPERS ON PERCH LAKE MOUNTAIN VANISH

We Come in Peace: Part 2 of a 2-Part Investigation

After encountering four adult campers near Shavertown Trail near Pepacton Reservoir, Roxbury guide Marvin Rogers listened to an incredible tale related by one of them, Ms. Kathy Young. Ms. Young, an astrophysicist and former Fox News science editor, maintained that she had been contacted by beings from the earth-like planet Keplar-62F in the Lyra constellation and, with the three other campers, expected to be "transmuted" into the stars in a matter of days.

This article continues the account told by Ms. Young to Marvin Rogers. That story is presented as a first-person narrative though in reality it is her account as told to Marvin who related it to this reporter.

According to Ms. Young:

"My conversation with Jack DeShannon, my old professor at Cal Tech, left me reeling. Someone at Keplar-62F, an earth-like planet 1,200 light-years away, had sent a message: my name spelled out in Morse code as dits and dahs picked up by a radio telescope. Whoever they were, they were for real.

"I took another look at the long email I had received, apparently from Keplar-62F. All the text was gone except for the GPS location where I should be on August 15. I copied the data and pasted it into Google. The location was a mountain near Andes, New York. Four or five clicks later, I pinpointed the location near what is called Shavertown Trail on Perch Lake Mountain.

"Should I or shouldn't I? How could I not? I went into my boss at Fox News and said I was going on a two-week leave on August 10. He said I couldn't, so I told him to kiss my butt and walked out.

"I went online and ordered camping equipment and did a little map reconnaissance. On August 14, I got a friend to drive me to the base of the Shavertown Trail near Pepacton Reservoir. I didn't bother to record my passing in the log at the start of the trail. I headed up and then used my GPS device to find the exact spot.

"Two tents were already pitched and two people were standing there.

"The three of us hugged. One was an astronomer named Cilia Black and the other an astrophysicist who did not give his name, but looked me in the eye and said, 'I always knew something like this would happen. I've been ready my whole life.'

"About two hours later another woman showed up. Barbara Lewis had been in astronaut training, but had resigned when it was obvious she wasn't going to be selected for a mission.

We talked for about four hours. All of us had studied astrophysics and astronomy, we were huge Dr. Who fans, and we all played geocaching games. All of us had grown up wanting to travel in space. Maybe we were going to have our chance."

At that point Ms. Young asked that Marvin leave, saying the campers wanted more time to talk among themselves.

Having heard the story, this reporter was more than a bit incredulous.

That night there was a tremendous Catskills lightning storm with thunder that echoed through the mountains. Marvin called me about 6:30 the next morning and said he was going to check on the campers. Did I want to go?

We had a quick breakfast in Roxbury and drove to the base of Shavertown Trail, parked, wrote in the log, and headed up at a fast pace.

About fifty minutes later we walked into the camp. No one was there. We called and called, but no one appeared.

The tents were all still up. I looked in two of them. Everything seemed to be there. Clothes, backpacks, an Arthur C. Clark novel, and an opened pack of Oreos.

In the middle of the camp were the propane stove and the solar generator, the latter with three cell phones hooked up. Ice chests still held food. There was no sign of anyone.

I gathered up the cell phones and checked them out. All had been wiped clean and all showed the time as 24:00, midnight.

Marvin and I looked at one another. There was not much to say.

Just then, a cell phone began to ring in one of the tents. We found it under a T-shirt with 'We Come in Peace" on it. Marvin said Kathy Young had been wearing it the day before.

I picked up the ringing phone. The time on it was 10:13 a.m., my birthday is October 13. I said, "Hello." No one was there.

36. CATSKILL ANIMALS IN THE NEWS

Bear Whisperer Goes Silent, Albany Not Concerned

A well-known bear whisperer sent by the New York Resources Development Administration to make contact with the Catskill's black bear population has disappeared. The man arrived in Halcott Center in mid-December planning to spend time in several bears' dens during the winter months.

The whisperer is said to be a Brooklyn hipster who began his interest in black bears (Ursus americanus) as a weekend-photographer in the Catskills. After several years, he became convinced that he could communicate with the animals and began to spend considerable time around adult bears.

A tracking device worn by the whisperer sent signals all winter, but the device stopped on April 2nd. Margaretville school kids who had been monitoring the whisperer's movements using a computer grew alarmed when the signals no longer were received.

The class's teacher immediately contacted Mr. Thomas Avatar, a supervisor at the New York Resources Development Administration (RDA). He replied that he was "not concerned. It is likely our whisperer's batteries just ran out. I bet he'll eventually show up. In the meanwhile, he's been placed on unpaid leave and someone has moved into his office."

When the new school year began this fall, Mr. Avatar was asked for an update. His lengthy email response contained several pages of legalese dealing with liability issues. The last paragraph included the information that as of two weeks ago, no one at the Resources Development Administration had heard from the individual. He remains on unpaid leave.

The RDA does not plan to employ any additional bear whisperers.

Bovina Duck Keeper Promises to Revolutionize Production of Foie Gras

A serendipitous discovery made by a Bovina dairy worker has drawn the attention of duck and geese farmers from France to Long Island. Three months ago, quite by accident, Ms. Mary Wells came up with a method to remove a large portion of a duck's liver without damaging the animal.

The innovation came about when Ms. Wells' duties expanded from helping care for dairy cattle to overseeing the feeding of ducks. One morning six ducks ate table scraps that Ms. Wells had left in a bucket next to the duck feed. The scraps were destined for a compost pile adjacent to the barn.

Several hours later, much to the amazement of Ms. Wells and the Bovina farmer who employed her, each of the six ducks each regurgitated a large portion of their liver. The next day none of the six seemed any the worse for wear.

It took Ms. Wells and the farmer several tries to reconstitute the table scrap recipe, but they were successful. Each member of the Bovina flock now is required to give up their paté-to-be once every other week. The feeding schedule calls for a fifth of the ducks to receive the special mixture—dubbed Ducks' Delight—each weekday (the ducks are given weekends off to swim in the farm pond). Amazingly, the ducks seem to be fitter and happier than they were before they were introduced to their new diet. Their livers quickly regenerate.

Though the farmer and milkmaid would not divulge the exact ingredients in Ducks' Delight for which a patent application has been submitted, they did say the blended mixture includes a number of locally available products, including garlic peels, gluten-free pancakes permeated with maple syrup, puree of cauliflower, locally harvested ginseng, and blueberry wine that is past its prime.

When asked about the exact source of the table scraps devoured by the original half dozen ducks, the farmer smiled and hinted it had something to do with a hearty farm breakfast.

According to the farmer, GlaxoSmithKline, a British pharmaceutical company, has an option on the potion and hopes to develop it as a non-invasive treatment for damaged livers in humans.

SPU Seeks to Organize Local Bovines

A half dozen representatives from the Society for the Protection of Ungulates (SPU) chapter based in New York City's Upper West Side have descended on farms across northern Delaware County. They hope to convince cows to join a labor union.

According to Bill Deal, lead organizer, "For far too long, cows have been treated, well, like cattle. Their remuneration is low, they endure long hours, and many have to sleep standing up. And chewing your cud all the time is not a very intellectually stimulating activity. We want to better their lives and their retirement years."

Mr. Deal, in an interview, admitted that thus far the SPU group had met few cows expressing a desire to unionize. "That is especially true of beef cattle, who seem to have little interest in planning for their senior years. Even the dairy cows had few complaints about their status, other than the early hours and cold milking machines. We were surprised.

"Our preliminary surveys suggest that rather than the cows having a harsh life, it is the farmers and their families who appear to have it the hardest. Our problem with organizing them, however, is that our attorneys cannot decide if farmers are management or labor."

37. BROOKLYN ENTREPRENEUR BACKING YET ANOTHER NEW LOCAL BUSINESS

Following on the heels of the collapse of Eskimo Heaven, his ill-fated fat freezing business in Stamford, Christian Potok, the self-proclaimed cowboy from the outer borough of Brooklyn, plans to open a video game arcade. Mr. Potok graciously took time to sit down with this reporter and talk about his plans for the new endeavor.

"Okay, I'll admit Eskimo Heaven flopped big time, but it was a great idea. It was just a bit too much for the Catskills. I bet in a few more years, every spa in the Catskills will be freezing fat. Can you imagine the bachelorette parties?

"But that is water under the bridge. This time, I've got a 'can't fail' idea: a place for the under-21 crowd who aren't allowed in bars to hang out after school. It's gonna have a real family-type atmosphere. My brother-in-law. Jake who just came home from eighteen months in Elmira, came up with the notion. He got a lot smarter in prison.

"Jake has some business contacts that hooked me up with a dozen almost-new video machines. We're going to move them into the old Eskimo Heaven building and set up a soda fountain and sell non-alcoholic Jell-O shots to the kids. We'll also have a pole so the kids can practice all those new dances."

When asked if the arcade will have a name, Mr. Potok replied, "That's the best part. Jake found Jesus while he was incarcinated (editor's note: it was pointed out to Mr. Potok that he likely meant "incarcerated," but he insisted incarcinated was correct)."

Mr. Potok went on, "I asked Jake to look in the Bible and see if he couldn't come up with a name or two that had a lot of history that would make Roxbury parents happy to give their kids money to spend at our arcade.

"Jake did some research and came up with Sodom and Gomorrah. He thinks they probably were the names of two Irish apostles or something like that. I hopped on the idea.

"Both names sure work as toasts with Jell-O shots. Can you picture it? 'Gomorrah! Bottoms up!' The kids will love it. What a place, huh?"

Mr. Potok hopes to have the grand opening for Sodom and Gomorrah Fun Arcade in about two weeks. He pointed out that no liquor license was required.

Breaking News: Sodom and Gomorrah Shuttered

Roxbury's newest business has been closed by state of New York authorities. Sodom and Gomorrah, a gaming parlor with snack bar and meant to draw teenagers, was the latest failed local brainchild of self-proclaimed Brooklyn cowboy Christian Potok.

Mr. Potok was adamant that the presence of several slot machines in the establishment was not his fault. "My brother-in-law, Jake, arranged for what I thought were computer games for kids. Things like 'Benny the Butcher' and 'Zombie Killers,' you know, games that are suitable for youngsters. I didn't know that some of the machines were used for gambling."

"Now that I've been busted, I can't get any license to open a new business. But Jake, who used to run an operation recycling grease from hamburger joints, before he was sentenced to Elmira, is going to open a new restaurant in this space."

In a subsequent interview with this reporter, Mr. Potok's brother-in-law Jake announced that the new restaurant would be called Yo Mama's Yokohama Yakitori. He stated the menu "is being developed by a friend from Puerto Rico that got blasted to Miami by that hurricane. We plan to open in the New Year."

When asked what entrees might be found on the forthcoming Yakitori menu, Jake declined to answer, saying he was waiting for the "guy to get here from Miami. He's down there researching it. But whatever it is, with that name, we know it will sell. We're expecting huge crowds—and it is going to be 'bring your own bottle.' We can't get a liquor license—too many priors on my arrest record."

Follow-up: After several failed business ventures in the Western Catskills, Mr. Potok has once again taken up fulltime residence in the Borough of Queens in New York City. Presently he is a Republican candidate for the New York State Assembly. In a brief telephone interview, he stated, "All that mountain stuff is behind me. I'm back to my roots. People here understand me."

38. BUSINESS ASSOCIATION OF ROXBURY TO SPONSOR MODIFIED FORMULA 1-TYPE AUTO RACE

Always eager to bring visitors to the Catskills, the Roxbury Business Coalition announced yesterday that the small community will soon turn itself into "Indianapolis for a Day." The First Annual Roxbury Gala 100 Road Race will be held Thanksgiving weekend.

Ms. Dionne Ross, Business Coalition president, held a news conference to outline plans for the automobile competition, which will "draw visitors and offer local drivers an opportunity to race around our streets without fear of a speeding ticket." The $25 entry fees will be used to promote Roxbury business, including subsidizing monthly Association cocktail get-togethers.

The Roxbury Gala 100 Road Race will take place over a 3.3-mile course. Starting and finishing lines are on Bridge Street in front of the WIOX radio station building. Racers will proceed in a counterclockwise direction south on Stratton Falls Road (Route 41) to the more than ninety-degree turn onto Briggs Road. The latter features a challenging S-shaped chicane and a narrow bridge. Cars will then navigate a ninety-degree left turn and accelerate north on the Route 30 straightaway into downtown Roxbury, where a right-angle left turn to the finish line challenges the drivers.

The one-hundred-mile-long race will entail thirty laps around the track. A handsome trophy will be awarded to the winner.

Ms. Ross expressed hope that next year the race would be expanded into an all-day event. "This first year we are going to have only one race. In subsequent years, we want to see three separate one-hundred-mile races; one for pickup trucks, one for cars, and the third for cars other than Subarus."

Businesses and residents adjoining the parking zone in front of Roxbury Wine and Spirits have graciously agreed to allow that area to be used for race cars to make pit stops (Note: there are no bathroom facilities available at that location; race drivers should make other plans).

Local authorities have mapped out a detour to keep regular traffic off Route 30 in downtown Roxbury the day of the race. The detour will follow Scudder Hill Road to Howard Greene Road, Grant Morse Road, and Vega Mountain Road. At the intersection of Vega Mountain Road and Route 30, a guide barrier will be erected, so that cars exiting Vega Mountain Route can turn north on Route 30 without impeding the race track.

Ms. Ross asked that advance media coverage of the race emphasize two points. First, the race is NOT a Demolition Derby. Also, drivers are asked not to practice driving the race course prior to the actual race, unless they do so at the legal speed limit.

Ms. Ross closed her remarks to the media by saying, "It will be a marvelous showcase for Roxbury. What could possibly go wrong?"

Another Business Association of Roxbury Initiative

Ms. Dionne Ross, BAR president, today released a list of podcasts created by the association to help new residents to the area adjust to life in the Catskills. All of the podcasts are online and can be accessed from any computer or smart phone.

Each podcast is approximately six minutes in length. Here is the list presently available:

- Learning to live with snow.

- Should I wash my car or not?

- Cell phones: who needs them anyway?

- Why cauliflower should be important in your diet.

- The driver in front: should I tailgate or not?

- Meeting new friends at the Transfer Station.

- Taco night or wings night? A guide to local dining.

- To rake or not to rake.

- Tractors and fire trucks: why seasonal parades look the same.

- Gardening for two: you and deer.

- My crap could be your crap: the Catskill tradition of holiday yard sales.

- Ironed clothes? Laundered clothes? What not to wear in the Catskills.

- Bear facts: Mama, they're so cute! Can I pet them?

39. RACE A HUGE SUCCESS

Several Drivers Go Off-Track; A Surprise Winner

The Friday after Thanksgiving brought fast cars (and trucks) to the roads of Roxbury for the "First Annual Gala 100 Road Race." Sponsored by the Business Association of Roxbury the race was billed as a Formula 1-like competition. The one-hundred-mile event certainly lived up to its name—at one point a 2015 Subaru Impreza was clocked with a speed gun at nearly fifty miles an hour.

As previously reported in this paper, the race began in front of the WIOX radio station, then went counterclockwise down Stratton Falls Road, across Briggs Road with its narrow bridge, left (north) on Route 30, then left again at Bridge Street to the start/finish line in front of WIOX's studios. The course is 3.3 miles long and the race was thirty laps.

Twenty cars and trucks were drawn by lot to participate in the race. Promptly at 10:55 a.m. the well-known host of a WIOX sports talk show told the drivers to "start your engines" and then watched as the pace car (the Roxbury Volunteer Fire Department's black and red pickup truck) led one unscored lap around the track.

The green flag was waved and the race was off. One car—a 2007 Hyundai—blew an engine only 500 yards from the starting line.

The race was without incident through the first seven laps. As the field approached the railroad crossing on Stratton Falls Road on lap eight, race organizers realized they had forgotten one important detail: the Delaware & Ulster Railroad train bringing tourists from

Arkville. Right on schedule, the morning train reached the crossing at 11:21 a.m.

The two lead cars cut left to miss the train and ended up in a field soaked by the rain-swollen East Branch of the Delaware River. Behind them the next cars hit their brakes, setting off a chain reaction that knocked eleven racers (nine cars and two pickups) out of the competition amidst smashed vehicles and foul language.

The six remaining cars continued the race. Two more were lost when they sideswiped one another trying to cross the Briggs Road Bridge at the same time. To the delight of the crowd, the less than a handful of cars left dueled every straightaway and curve the rest of the one hundred miles.

When the checked flag was waved, the winner turned out to be a 2014 Morris Mini Cooper. The excited crowd clapped and cheered when the driver spun two donuts in front of the Roxbury Motel before shutting the car down.

That is when the biggest surprise of the day occurred. The driver turned out to be a fourteen-year old Roxbury Central School student who lived in Grand Gorge.

The young woman's first words upon exiting the driver's seat were, "Please don't tell my parents! They're in Cooperstown for the day visiting relatives. If they find out I drove Mom's car again, I'll be grounded for life. If I thought I might win, I wouldn't have done it."

Business Association organizers promise a bigger and better race day next year, with plans already underway for three separate contests: Subarus, cars other than Subaru (OTS), and pickup trucks. The first race will begin about 11:30 in the morning, well after the Delaware & Ulster train has arrived in Roxbury.

40. CONSTABLE'S CORNER— CRIME IN THE CATSKILLS

T he *Catskill Tribune* presents its second "Constable's Corner" col- umn, a report on an ugly incident in our community perpetrated by outside agitators.

Birthday Party Surprise Flattens Rude Bachelor Party Attendees

When a brawl erupted at a local bar and grill last Friday, there was no need to call in the United States Marines. She was already there. Locals who witnessed the melee will talk about it for years.

The evening started out on a bad note when ten Brooklyn hip- sters showed up for a previously scheduled bachelor party and be- gan to make snide comments about other customers. The bartender told this reporter that all the young men had been drinking heavily before they arrived and continued ordering cocktails and shots of liqueur after they were seated.

On the opposite side of the room were a dozen women celebrat- ing the birthday of a colleague. Unbeknownst to the honoree, who was turning fifty-five, her friends had constructed a six-foot high paper-mâché rocket decorated with red, white, and blue crepe paper and the slogan "Soaring into Middle Age."

Inside the rocket was a birthday surprise: the woman's daughter who had come home on leave from her posting as a marine in Afghanistan where she had won her unit's Tae Kwon Do championship.

The rocket was wheeled in on a large mechanic's creeper. Before the daughter could pop out to surprise her mother, one of the hipsters thought it would be great fun to pretend the rocket was a piñata. He picked up a mop from the back room and took two swings, hitting the rocket both times. He never had a chance for a third.

The marine tore through the side of the rocket, grabbed the mop, and broke the end off over the man's head. She then snapped the mop handle over a knee and used the two pieces to firmly rap both sides of the guy's head simultaneously. That was followed by a sharp kick to the groin. The disabled attacker, who was in disbelief that a female demon wearing a black cocktail dress and heels had emerged from the piñata, fell prone on the floor.

At that point a brief melee ensued. Three of the other bachelor party attendees ran at the marine and took swings at her. She did a pirouette in her high heels and felled the trio in rapid succession with two kicks and a straight punch to the chest. One tried to get up, but received a kick in the solar plexus for his effort.

There was a pause in the action while the hipsters regrouped. Two of them then rushed the marine, one armed with a chair. They didn't last long. The marine disarmed the man with the chair and then flattened him with a spinning back fist. She next broke the chair over the other assailant.

With six of their number down, the remainder of the hipsters decided it was time to retreat. They exited through the back door.

The bartender calmly took the wallet out of the back pocket of one of the dazed men lying on the floor and used a credit card to pay their bill, the tip, and the damage to the mop and chair. After the wallet and card were returned, the injured men were unceremoniously escorted out the front door to the jeers of the Roxbury regulars sitting at the bar.

According to one onlooker, "The action was as good as anything you would ever see in one of those Bruce Lee movies. If that first guy that got kicked in the crotch had been a football, she would have made a forty-five-yard field goal with him."

The marine was given a standing ovation and the entire crowd sang Happy Birthday to her mother.

By the time the town constable arrived, all was calm. The constable was given a piece of birthday cake for his trouble.

"Kung Fu Night" was such a success that the owner of the bar and restaurant is considering showing Kung Fu movies one night a week, while featuring a special Asian-themed meal.

41. NAKED FORCE ON DISPLAY IN ULSTER COUNTY HAMLET

It was Nudists versus Buddhists at a public lecture in the Pine Hill Community Center last Saturday. William Haley, Professor of Religion at the State University of New York in Delhi, thought something was amiss when he took the lectern for his afternoon talk. Expecting twenty people at most in the audience, he found a standing-room only crowd of well over 150.

Handbills advertising Dr. Hale's address, entitled "A Penetrating Look at Buddhists in the Catskills: Finding Peace in Nature," had been posted in towns along Route 28 from Arkville to Olive. Several Onteora High School students from Boiceville, bent on having some pre-Halloween fun, had used sharpies to alter many of the signs to read "A Penetrating Look at Nudists in the Catskills."

About five minutes into Professor Haley's erudite presentation a woman in the audience stood up and asked "When do we get to take our clothes off?" That was followed by a man with a Rip Van Winkle-like white beard who chimed in, "Yeah, I didn't drive all the way here from Frost Valley to hear about church."

A number of people in the audience began to strip. One couple stood up on their folding chairs and began to disrobe. With her pants down around her ankles the woman lost her balance and fell forward atop one of two Buddhists monks who were sitting in the next row. The monk pulled his saffron robe off and tried to cover the woman. Under his robe the monk was wearing only a pair of orange Speedo briefs.

As members of the audience pressed close, the monk and the woman tussled on the floor. The woman's partner tried to kick the nearly naked Buddhist, but could not get a clear shot because of all the chairs. The second monk, who had taken vows of non-violence but still had spent considerable time watching television reruns of David Carradine portraying a Shaolin monk in the 1970s series Kung Fu, began executing martial arts moves.

At that point Professor Haley pulled a fire alarm, which set off cries of "Fire" and a mass exodus out the front door. A local business owner, seeing a mob of half-naked people running down Main Street, began to scream "Zombies! Zombies!"

A restauranteur grabbed a shotgun she kept on a shelf under her cash register and fired two shots over the heads of what she thought was an invasion of godless, flesh-devouring zombies, adding to the panic.

Several high school students were observed standing in front of the community center watching the bedlam and laughing hysterically, their cell phones recording the scene.

After volunteer firemen arrived and calmed the crowd, small groups of people were allowed to take turns going back into the building to retrieve clothing and other items. Seven people were treated for exposure.

A tourist from New Jersey traveling through Pine Hill observed, "I never expected to see anything like this along the Catskill Mountains Scenic Byway. Do they have a Naked Zombie Invasion every Halloween? They might want to mention it in the guidebook."

42. NEWS OF INTEREST FROM THE WESTERN CATSKILLS

A farmer on Roses Brook Road southwest of South Kortright was cutting down dead corn stalks to fashion Thanksgiving decorations, when what he thought was a pumpkin-sized meteor landed almost on top of him. He later described the object as "glowing green and smelling like a mixture of scotch whiskey and room deodorizer." The farmer thought it likely the comet was an emerald from outer space.

With visions of dollar signs dancing in his head, the farmer placed the object in a fifty-five-gallon drum, loaded the drum into the back of his pickup truck, secured everything with bungee cords, and, with his daughter as a passenger, headed for the Department of Astronomy at SUNY-Delhi. Speeding down Route 10, he could not help dreaming about how he would spend what the heavens had bestowed on him.

In Delhi, the tarp was pulled back to reveal the emerald. But all that was in the drum was about eight gallons of greenish liquid. One professor surmised that the "comet" was frozen waste from a leaking bathroom tank on a jet landing at Stewart Airport in Newburgh. Delta flight 4281 from Detroit, a CRJ200, landed at Stewart Airport in Newburgh at 1:37 p.m. that afternoon, about the time the frozen mass had dropped.

With his dreams of a fortune melted, the disappointed farmer headed home, stopping just outside Bloomville to empty the drum beside the road. His equally disappointed daughter later told this reporter, "Well, at least it didn't land on his truck."

Secret Service Raids Delaware County Conservative Group

A Halloween night party sponsored by a Delaware County political party and attended by nearly forty people ended in chaos. Guests were taken into custody by United States Secret Service agents and held for more than seventy-two hours.

The costume event had a horror show theme. About half of the guests came as Freddy Krueger of the Nightmare on Elm Street film series, including wearing a glove with long (fake) razors attached. Other guests donned hockey goalie masks and carried chainsaws.

Officials had paid for placards to be printed up, each reading, "Trump Is A Friend," which party goers held for a group photograph.

Unfortunately, the printer had misspelled "Friend." By the time anyone noticed, photographs had hit social medium portraying more than three dozen seemingly maniacal killers each carrying a sign proclaiming, "Trump is a Fiend." The photos went viral.

The Facebook postings drew immediate attention from the secret service. Thinking the group could be a terrorist sect based in the rural Catskill Mountains, who were bent on assassinating the president, an elite strike force was dispatched within minutes. As the last twenty partygoers were about to head home, agents wearing black balaclava-type ski masks rappelled down ropes from two VH-60 Black Hawk helicopters and shot everyone with Tasers. Guests were bound with plastic ties, hooded, and taken by helicopter to a secure location in Langley, Virginia, where they were held incommunicado.

On Saturday morning, November 4, all twenty were released and given bus tickets to Kingston, with transfers to the flag stop near Fair

Street in Margaretville. The return trip to Delaware County took eighteen hours. On arriving home, seven of the individuals threatened to become Democrats and one said she would register as a member of the Catskills First Party.

Party organizers agreed that next year their Halloween gala would have a Cinderella/Prince Charming theme.

Walking Catfish Waylay Truck

A potato chip delivery truck driving from Grand Gorge to Roxbury overturned on Route 30 north of the Roxbury Transfer Station last week. The driver claimed he swerved to avoid several walking catfish that were crossing the road against traffic.

A check with an ichthyologist at the State University of New York in Oneonta verified the claim of walking catfish (Clarias batrachus) in the headwaters of the East Branch of the Delaware River. "Perhaps someone released the catfish, which they originally acquired in Florida to keep as pets. But they do lousy in aquarium, because they can simply walk away. In Florida they have been known to hitchhike long distances to find a mucky, slow-moving water source, their preferred habitat."

The scientist went on to say: "Here in the Catskills, we don't expect the catfish to become a threat to local species. Cold weather likely will take care of the problem. In the meanwhile, if you see walking catfish trying to get a ride south for the winter, don't pick them up."

43. VIKINGS IN THE CATSKILLS?

Four hikers from Norway have made an extraordinary discovery etched in a boulder on private land near Esopus Creek, east of Slide Mountain in Ulster County. Stopping to rest, the vacationers noticed five-centimeter-high Old Norse runes deeply carved into what a geologist subsequently said was shale rock from the Late Devonian Epoch.

The runes appear to read "Thjørson 967." Next to the runes is an X-like Norse symbol thought to represent Gibu Auja, the Viking Bringer of Good Luck.

Experts at the University of Oslo in Norway who were contacted about the runes initially expressed doubt that Vikings had traveled as far south as the Catskill Mountains. But after consulting a detailed map of the region, they said it was possible that Vikings intent on exploring and establishing trading partners among Native Americans may have reached the area.

Professor Bjorn Olafson of the Department of Viking and Medieval Norse Studies surmised that a party of Vikings traveled by sea from a settlement in Newfoundland down the Atlantic coast to New York Harbor. Finding the Hudson River, they followed it north to see if it connected with the St. Lawrence River. Such a route would have provided Viking traders and raiders with an inland passage to and from the Gulf of St. Lawrence and the new Viking settlements in that vast region.

Professor Olafson conjectures that Vikings sailing in longboats up the Hudson River may have stopped near modern Saugerties in Green County and then sent a scout party up Esopus Creek. That stream took them south, then southwest, then north to near Slide Mountain where the runes were discovered. After marking their passage with runes carved in a boulder, the Vikings retraced their route.

Over the last several decades, three Viking archaeological sites dating about one thousand years ago have been found in Newfoundland (L'Anse aux Meadows, Sop's Arm, and Point Rosee). Norse sagas mention "Helluland" (likely modern-day Baffin Island), "Markland" (Labrador), and "Vinland" (perhaps Newfoundland or a land farther south). Together the archaeological evidence and the sagas suggest a much greater Viking presence in northeastern North America than once thought.

News of the runes has swept through the village of Boiceville and the surrounding town of Olive. People are genuinely excited that Vikings once visited their region. Students at the Onteora High School are voting next week to change their school mascot from Eagles (selected in 2016 when the name Indians was dropped) to Vikings.

Olive town officials are in the throes of planning a gala Viking festival for the fall and already have made contact with Stavenger, Norway, to set up a sister city program. According to one official who is a candidate for public office, "We expect Vikings to lead us into a new era of prosperity. Once known as pillagers, the Vikings now have the opportunity to atone for their past by brightening our future."

Not all Boiceville residents are as optimistic. Several residents shopping at a well-known local bakery thought the news was too good to be true. One opined, "How in hell could Vikings have found this place? We can't even get tourists with google maps on iPhones to come here."

Breaking News—Vikings Naysayers Vindicated

Just as we were going to press this morning, seventy-five-year-old Tom Ericson, a lifetime Boiceville resident, called in with news that will cast a pall over Olive.

Mr. Ericson asked, "Was that carving everyone is talking about on an eight-foot-tall boulder twenty-five feet or so west of the Esopus? My dad and I carved that rock during hunting season in 1955. That was the year I got my first buck. I was twelve that day. To commemorate it, dad carved "Thom & Son 1955" on a big rock. Then I put an X by it to mark the spot. My dad, Thomas, liked to use the name Thom. He said it gave him a little bit more class. Tom is good enough for me, so I use that name. I would have told you it wasn't any Vikings, if anybody had asked."

44. ROXBURY SKI CENTER TO GO GREEN THIS WINTER

Thanks to a grant from the New York State Division of Tourism, Roxbury's local ski center will literally be going green this winter. Funding was received for a unique initiative: dying the snow on the ski slopes green.

Tourism officials hope that green snow attracts another kind of green: money spent in the community by winter visitors.

At a meeting of ski center officials, local business people, and tourism representatives held in November at the ski center's charming lodge, plans were finalized for the Go Green undertaking. Using the latest technology, a coloring agent will be added to snow-making equipment to turn the generated snow crystals green. Grant funds will subsidize the purchase of the hundreds of barrels of dye that will be used over the winter.

At the meeting there was considerable discussion over which color to use on the slopes. A secret ballot was held in which voters could choose among the primary colors. Green won by a landslide. A second balloting then took place to select the exact shade of green. Lime green was the unanimous choice.

According to one tourism official, "Lime green will be THE color of the upcoming ski season in Roxbury. We are hoping for lime green skis, ski attire, and anything else anyone can think of."

On St. Patrick's Day, Saturday March 17, the ski center will have a special feature: a booth in which skiers can have themselves and their underwear sprayed lime green before slaloming down the slopes. A representative declared that anyone skiing green in their green undies will have to be over eighteen years of age and pass a sobriety test prior to each trip down mountain. It was noted, however, that if the snow and the skier were the same color, it is unlikely anyone would notice the individual anyway.

45. LIFE AND LOVE IN THE CATSKILLS

The *Catskill Tribune* is pleased to present a special holiday, "Life and Love in the Catskills" column. In the last few weeks our "Life and Love" mail box has been inundated with letters that are variations on the theme "angst for the holidays" and seeking advice regarding relatives and revelry, or lack thereof. Our "Life and Love" editor has selected two letters that typify many of those that were received.

TO THE LIFE AND LOVE EDITOR: The holidays are coming and I am seriously considering drinking myself into a stupor and passing out in the snow, never to awake. It is my sister. Once again, she is driving up from Baltimore to help me "celebrate" the Winter solstice (I don't even know when it is, but she does—she doesn't do Christmas). She has fifteen-year-old female Goth twins that are absolute terrors and listen to loud emo music day and night. Even my dogs are scared of them. My sister hates men (of which I am one) and insists the twins are the result of a virgin birth. Last year for the solstice, she and the twins dressed up in robes and did what they said were Druid dances around a pole they put up in my front yard. Some were pretty obscene. The neighbors called the cops. I cooked and cleaned up after the three of them for what seemed like weeks. I can't face them again this year. Please help!

(Signed) Desperate to Dodge the Druids

DEAR DESPERATE: Call your sister (or send an email) and explain that you have been asked by old friends to spend the holidays at Stonehenge in England. She'll understand. Then buy a plane ticket to London, check into a grand hotel, and have a wonderful time. The expense will be worth it. By the way, the Winter solstice is December 21.

TO THE LIFE AND LOVE EDITOR: Anxiety. That is what Hanukkah means to me. The problem is my mother. She is planning to fly in from LA to visit me in Roxbury to celebrate and intends to stay ALL EIGHT DAYS!!!! It gets worse. Mother is going to bring her latest husband (Husband #4), Ronnie, who is at least twenty-five years younger than Mother, which makes him two years younger than me. I met him once and I am certain he is gay. He is a loser who has never held a job in his life. He's also a gluten-free vegan and I think he voted for Trump. It gets worse. She and Ronnie want to stay here in the spare bedroom in our two-bedroom town house. I may slit my wrists. It gets worse. Mother thinks that my wife, Jessie, whom she has not yet met, is a female. He's not. Jesse is his real name and two months ago we eloped to Lake Placid, which thankfully is far, far away from LA. I have never come out to her. She doesn't know I am gay. It gets worse. Jesse and I always have a big Christmas tree—Mother wants a menorah. I can't find one for sale around here, but I guess I could order one from Amazon. Jesse, the sweetheart, says he can move out for the week that Mother is here—he also has offered to stay, but go in drag the whole time. I am a complete wreck!!! What should I do????

(Signed) Hot Mess for the Holidays

DEAR HOT MESS: Wow! Boy, do you need a plan (by the way, I think you can probably get a menorah at the General Store in Roxbury). First, call Mother and explain your situation. Maybe start by telling her you think Ronnie is gay, but emphasize that it is OK. Get her on the defensive. Then slip in that your spouse is also gay. She should be able to figure the rest out on her own. Next, make up some big lie about the state of the spare bedroom. In fact, get rid of the furniture and paint part of the room some horrible color; remove the light fixtures and wall socket covers. Tell her she and Ronnie would not be comfortable staying with you, because the spare room is being renovated. Suggest, no insist, she stay at The Roxbury in one of the theme suites. Ronnie will love it, and so will you. Another tactic is to pray for snow that would cause her flight to be canceled or would at least delay her arrival for a few days. Also, if you go online, I'm sure you can find a Hebrew prayer for bad weather. Lastly, arrange to volunteer at some facility that is helping to feed people over the holidays. Take Mother and Ronnie. They probably won't last long and might fly back to LA early. Have a Happy Hanukkah!

46. DEVELOPERS CONFIDENT PLANS FOR ICE PALACE WON'T MELT

Anyone who can built an indoor ski slope in a gargantuan shopping mall in a desert should have no problem developing an underground ice-skating rink, shopping mall, and hotel in the Catskills. That is the ambitious plan outlined two days ago at a press conference in Kingston.

Citizens and members of the media who attended the briefing were awestruck by the scope and meticulous planning behind the multi-million-dollar development, not to mention the gargantuan funding.

Financial backing and project oversight are being provided by two huge Middle East companies headquartered in Dubai, the largest and most populous city in the United Arab Emirates.

Emaar Properties, one of the project backers, developed the world-famous Dubai Mall with its indoor skating rink. Emaar has teamed up with the Majid Al Futtaim Group, the company that built and owns the Mall of the Emirates, the largest mall in the world in terms of area. Mall of the Emirates, also in Dubai, features an indoor ski slope. The family of the late Sultan of Oman, Qaboos bin Said al Said, is also one of the Catskill project's investors.

The site selected for the Ulster County underground mall is extraordinary. About three years ago, the nephew of the Sultan of Oman visited Roxbury and picked up a copy of a book on the region (The

Catskills in the Ice Age, 2003 revised edition), written by famed Catskill geologist Robert Titus.

The nephew was excited by mention of a rock-lined "chimney" leading down from the ground surface to the top of a permanent ice strata. Reaching down into the chimney one could actually touch a remnant of the Ice Age (Pleistocene Epoch) glacier that covered the Catskill Mountains until about 15,000 years ago.

The young Omani man located and visited the chimney, which is not all that far from Peekamoose restaurant in Big Indian, Ulster County. Having grown up in a desert on the Arabian Peninsula, the man became fascinated with the possibility of using the natural cold of the subsurface stratum for a unique development.

Subsequent drilling showed that the underground ice formation, insulated for more than fifteen millennia by rock formations, is extensive, covering at least several acres.

Over an eighteen-month period the developers quietly bought up the underground rights to the land north of Rondout Creek containing the ice stratum. They plan to "mine" a portion of the ice, leaving a significant amount that will be used for a year-round ice-skating rink.

Around the ice rink there will be a subterranean 150-room theme resort based on the 2013 Walt Disney animated movie Frozen that recently was made into a Broadway show. There also will be stores, restaurants, and a bingo parlor.

Because the complex will be managed by an American-based company, the complex will include several lounges serving alcohol, one of which will be an adult ice bar featuring famed exotic pole dancer, Glacier Moraine from Duluth, Minnesota.

A host of attorneys and engineers from New York City were on hand to answer questions after the presentation by a representative of the developers. Many of the questions centered on the permits that would be required to build the ambitious development. Some in the audience cited the more than decade-long battle to build the Belleayre Resort complex that, according to a recent editorial in the Catskill Mountain News was "stymied by government bureaucracy and frivolous lawsuits."

Though some in the audience were skeptical the project will ever see fruition, the developers' legal team was confident they would have few problems in moving forward. The attorneys pointed out that many of the present laws and regulations are geared towards above-ground development and do not apply to underground construction.

They emphasized that the planned Ice Palace complex, as it has been tentatively named, will be a self-contained, subsurface bio-center. The complex will feature a closed recycling system for water and sewage. It also will generate its own electricity. Supplies and workers, as well as guests, will be brought in by underground trams that will carry trash and departing staff and guests out. The lead project attorney opined, "People will be able to walk over the complex and not even know that it is below them. Who would ever be opposed to such a development, one that promises prosperity for the Catskill Mountains?"

47. A CHRISTMAS STORY: ROXBURY WOMAN BRINGS PATERNITY SUIT AGAINST JOLLY OLD ELF

Claiming that Santa Claus fathered her three-month-old son, a resident on Vega Mountain Road has retained a team of Margaretville attorneys to file a lawsuit against St. Nicholas. The suit seeks both acknowledgment of paternity and child support.

Merrie Holidaze, a pseudonym the woman is using to conceal her identity, claims she was impregnated by Mr. Kringle on Christmas Eve 2017 after he came down her chimney. According to Ms. Holidaze, "I was overwhelmed by the presence of such an illustrious personage and easily succumbed to his wiles. The only other well-known person I had ever met previously was a judge that I had to appear before in Poughkeepsie when I was studying English literature in college and got busted."

She went on to say "I had just commenced hanging up my stocking on Christmas Eve when out of nowhere Santa Claus appeared on the scene. We shared a couple of cups of pumpkin eggnog I'd bought at an after-Thanksgiving sale in Roxbury. Then we smoked a little and sang along with Eartha Kitt's version of Santa Baby.

"One thing led to another and in no time that sly elf had seduced me. Worse was that a couple of reindeer watched through a window.

"The next day I wasn't certain if it had been an eggnog-and-rum-in-duced dream or if Santa had actually been there. But by Valentine's Day I knew I was with child. He sure left me a holiday present.

"I wrote a sheaf of letters to the North Pole, but never received a response. Little Johnny is now over a year old and it is time Mr. Claus took some responsibility for his son, who is not all that jolly."

Ms. Holidaze's attorneys declined to comment on the case, beyond noting that they had filed extradition requests with all the countries claiming a piece of the North Pole.

This past week rumors abounded that there was a plan afoot to have Mr. Claus taken into custody when he appeared in mid-December in the Roxbury Holiday Parade or afterward at the Roxbury firehouse where he was to pose with children for photographs. That story led to a protest march the afternoon before the parade at the attorneys' Margaretville offices.

At the protest several young demonstrators carried posters on which was printed, "U R GRINCHES." Four eight-year-olds held a giant banner decorated with holiday motifs and demanding, "NO ARREST FOR SANTA CLAUS UNTIL AFTER WE GET OUR PRESENTS! WHERE IS YOUR XMAS SPIRIT?"

Neither Santa nor his elves were apprehended at the Roxbury holiday gala. Roxbury's assistant fire chief released a statement before the parade saying "No way are we going to have anything to do with screwing up Christmas. We are also keeping an eye out for anyone at the parade or the firehouse who looks suspicious and might be planning to grab Mr. Claus."

Apparently, there were so many people at the event who were deemed shifty-looking by fire department officials that firemen from Grand Gorge and Arkville were called in to help spot troublemakers. As it turned out, all the individuals being shadowed were local Delaware County residents.

Ms. Holidaze had no comment on the plot to nab Santa Claus. She told this reporter that she intends to spend the holiday season with little Johnny at her new boyfriend's house in Kingston. Chris, the boyfriend, is presently working as a mall Santa Claus. With a twinkle in her eye, Ms. Holidaze quipped "I've always been attracted to men in red."

48. MAKING THE CATSKILLS A BETTER PLACE TO LIVE

Suggestions from Our Readers

With a new year just around the corner the *Catskill Tribune* dispatched several interns into the hollows and byways of the region to check the pulse of the public. What suggestions did residents have to improve our lives here in the "Mountains of Love?" Here are a few of the responses.

Multiple individuals mentioned the need for cellular phone service in the small burg of Roxbury. As one young woman noted, "They can even use cell phones in Arkville!"

More than a handful of people called for "less broccoli in restaurants." One person added this caveat: "unless the broccoli is steamed, then sautéed with garlic. Grilled broccoli doesn't do it for me."

Other multiple responses were (in no particular order): more hiking and biking trails, more trains for tourists to ride, more jobs, lower property and school taxes, and better funded schools.

Beyond this litany of oft proposed ideas were some that are unique. One long-time resident of Halcottsville, who pointed out that her family had lived there for seven generations opined, "We're sorely in need of a stoplight at the intersection in the middle of town where Halcottsville Road and Bragg Hollow Road intersect." She went on to note, "Twice last week I counted seven cars at one time driving near that dangerous intersection. Worse traffic jam I've ever seen in town and I've lived here since FDR was president (God rest his soul). He saved America after the

Great Depression, but where is he when we need him?"

Two other Halcottsville residents suggested dredging Lake Wawaka. "The town could sell all that muck as fertilizer. And people would flock here to see what sort of things there might be down in the silt. For years there have been rumors about missing people and even cars. When Jimmy Hoffa disappeared in 1975, there were a lot of weird bubbles coming up from the lake bottom for a couple of weeks."

Up Vega Mountain Road, one of our interns stopped to speak with a man who had driven his car into a ditch. His suggestion for improving life in the Catskills was to "give pets last names. It's degrading for a pet to only have a first name. Hell, pets are like people to a lot of folks around here. We ought to be treating them better."

Veronica "Ronnie" Bennett of Margaretville was very emphatic about what she thought the northwestern Catskills needed: "More action! We need bars, places to dance, activities that would bring crowds to our little towns. Let's think big. How about a reality show? I bet a show that featured a commune of cheesemakers or something like that would make the whole world aware of what a neat place we have in the Catskills."

Ms. Bennett may be on to something. There are rumors that television people have been scouting locations and story angles around Bovina, South Kortright, and Hobart for a reality television show. Be assured that the *Catskill Tribune* will be following the story.

49. NEWS FROM THE WESTERN CATSKILLS

After the huge success of the "First Annual Gala 100 Road Race," the Business Association of Roxbury is underwriting a college football extravaganza. The inaugural Kirkside Cauliflower Kickoff Bowl is tentatively scheduled for mid-December of next year.

At a news conference originally to be held outdoors in Kirkside Park, but moved indoors due to frigid weather, a spokesperson for the Association outlined the thinking behind the forthcoming game. "After watching a number of taped college bowl games from the 2017-2018 bowl season, Roxbury's business leaders are convinced there is a place for a new approach to football bowl games. I mean, look at the Boca Raton Bowl between Florida Atlantic University and Akron on December 19. The stands were so empty you could have run a herd of dairy cattle through the place and not hit a spectator. Final score was 50-3 in favor of FAU. By the middle of the third quarter even the bands had left.

"Then there was the December 22 Popeye's Bahama Bowl: Ohio 41, University of Alabama-Birmingham 6. The cheerleaders departed with two of the referees at half time, headed for a tiki bar on the beach. There were fewer people in the stands than there were at the bar! And don't forget the famous Idaho Potato Bowl with the Central Michigan Chippewas against the Wyoming Cowboys also on December 22. Boring! Even some of the players were napping by the end of the first half.

"Our Kirkside Cauliflower Kickoff Bowl will be the first game of next year's bowl season and we will bring a new concept to team selection. Instead of two mismatched mediocre teams we will feature two total losers. We intend to have teams that have not won a game all season, teams with 0-11 records. What excitement!

"The Cauliflower Bowl will build winners. A team that has failed all year will emerge victorious. We hope to instill an 'anything-is-possible' spirit in the youth of America!"

Local activities planned for team players during the week-long run-up to the game include a cauliflower cook-off and a BB gun contest with blow-up Christmas yard decorations as targets. There also will be a contest to see which team's players can drink the most maple syrup and eat the most apples.

According to the Business Association spokesperson, "Teams that have been facing soul-sapping adversity all fall will clamor to be in the Kirkside Cauliflower Kickoff Bowl and experience winter in the north, while seeking redemption for a season gone south. We are presently seeking NCAA permission for the bowl and we are putting together our team of sponsors. This could be the biggest thing to hit our area in a long time."

Christmas Cat Flattens Grand Gorge Granny

Usually a time of joyous tidings, this holiday season brought bad news to one local woman. The day after Christmas, a resident of Grand Gorge suffered injuries when the woman's Christmas tree fell on top of her.

On Wednesday night after Christmas, Roseanna Hicks was sitting next to the decorated tree playing with a kitten that had been given to her as a present. The cat, whose name was Sparky, decided to climb the tree, knocking it over on top of Ms. Hicks. The huge cast iron star on the tree's top—a family heirloom—hit Ms. Hicks on the head, causing her to see stars. A number of the tree lights broke, tripping a circuit breaker, but not before administering an electrical shock to Ms. Hicks who had been knocked flat by the falling tree.

Regaining consciousness, Ms. Hicks activated a medical alert bracelet that her son had just given her for Christmas. A monitor in Albany immediately responded, asking Ms. Hicks if there was an emergency. She answered, "I've fallen and I can't get up. Also, I see a big star and a lot of little stars."

The monitor, thinking it was a crank call, quipped, "Don't call me; call the Three Wise Men and follow the biggest star." Ms. Hicks, who later managed to stand up by herself and reset the breaker in her fuse box, plans to sue the medical alert service.

50. NEW YEAR NEWS FROM THE WESTERN CATSKILLS

Two recent graduates of the New York University film school have set up a studio in Bovina called Hipster Heaven Films (HHFilms). The studio is backed in large part by a hedge fund run by the father of one of the founders of HHFilms.

HHFilms' initial project is a television reality show that will be filmed entirely in and around central Delaware County. The sixty-minute weekly show, tentatively entitled BABES, BROS, AND BOVINES, will focus on the trials, tribulations, and loves of four young Brooklynites—one man and three women—who move to the western Catskills to run a dairy farm. The four, none of whom have ever lived outside New York City and none of whom are professional actors, will rely solely on the internet for information about buying and breeding cattle, feeding the stock, and milk production. The farm will also feature a cheese-making operation and a roadside stand to sell dairy products.

In an interview with the *Catskill Tribune*, Barbara Madoff co-founder of HHFilms said, "We're going to show our television audience how four individuals from the big city, who know nothing about dairy farms and cheese, making can use Google and YouTube to find romance and profits."

At a public Question and Answer session held at a Hobart restaurant, Ms. Madoff emphasized that the intent of the show was a money-making operation within the "context of harmonious social relationships." She promised BABES, BROS, AND BOVINES "will serve as an archetype for anyone seeking to make a fortune in dairy farming, while finding passion and personal fulfillment."

In the Q&A, it became apparent to many local residents in attendance that Ms. Madoff and the four individuals who are to star in the show were remarkably uninformed about dairy farming. Two of the four believed chocolate milk came from brown cows. Another had no idea that dairy cows produced both male and female calves and that only female cows were milked. The fourth thought curds were an ethnic group living in the Middle Eastern. To say that some in the audience were skeptical of the venture would be an understatement.

When Ms. Madoff asked if anyone in the audience would be interested in investing in either the television show or the farm, there were no takers.

51. PEPACTON POLAR BEARS OPT OUT OF NEW YEAR'S DAY DIP

For more than three decades, a dedicated cadre of Catskill residents have met at dawn each January 1 near Shavertown Bridge for a clandestine skinny dip in Pepacton Reservoir. The forty or so members of the Pepacton Polar Bears span three generations.

The Polar Bears are especially proud of their unofficial slogan: "Furtive and Freezing." They are "Furtive," because swimming in the reservoir is not allowed; "Freezing" needs no explanation.

For thirty plus years, authorities have never halted the annual dash into the water and the group has never missed a New Year's Day date with Mother Nature. This year, however, Mother Nature brought a halt to the madcap stunt with a temperature of -8 degrees.

According to the keeper of the Polar Bears chronicles, only twelve members showed up at dawn on the first day of the year. The daring dozen had brave intentions, but upon discovering that all three containers of hot toddies needed to get their blood flowing were frozen, several Bears chose to watch from shore.

The rebellion set off a heated discussion on whether everyone should enter the water or not. Several of the skinny dippers, already stripped down to birthday suits, began to turn blue. Two other members who had waded into the water were shaking as though struck with some tropical palsy.

At that point, others of the group lost their nerve, despite a pep talk from their oldest member, who had never missed a New Year's swim in the annual escapade, when it originated a third of a century ago. A vote was taken and all but one person cast their ballot for going back to bed.

After more frosty debate, it was decided the Pepacton Polar Bears would return next year no matter the temperature, as long as there was not ice along the fringes of the reservoir.

At that point the Polar Bears made their ceremonial rite of urination in the reservoir. The ritual commemorates what many in the Catskill community still feel is the unfair inundation of Shavertown and other communities by the construction of the reservoir, a massive hydrological project undertaken to provide water for New York City. Members jocularly refer to the act of rebellion as the "Inundation Urination."

One Polar Bear opined, "It is too cold now to pee very much, but I'll be back when it's warmer to make my annual offering."

Roxbury's Big Melt

It was thought to be the World's Largest Tuna Melt, a sandwich that would garner international acclaim. Last weekend, the ears of a visiting Irish executive of Guinness, the famed stout maker founded in Dublin in 1759, perked up while dining at Chappie's Restaurant in Roxbury.

The administrator overheard several local residents at the next table discussing the "humungous melt" scheduled for spring following the Catskills' frigid winter. The Irishman, having enjoyed a number of gin and tonics, thought what was being talked about was plans for the world's largest tuna melt sandwich, not the annual thawing of ice and snow that signals the onset of the Catskills' mud season.

In no time at all the man, who was staying in Roxbury, was on his cell phone. The next week an advance crew from the Guinness Book of World Records landed at Stewart Airport outside Newburgh.

The Irish staff visited Chappie's, where they sought information about the gigantic tuna melt. The chef at Chappie's claimed no knowledge of the undertaking, referring the Irish producer and her aides to the Business Association of Roxbury. A representative of the association similarly denied any familiarity with a humungous sandwich.

Thwarted, the Guinness record book representatives left town, but not before hiring a local real estate agent of Irish descent to contact them, if more information were forthcoming.

In the meanwhile, the Business Association of Roxbury was quick to take advantage of the interest in the town shown by the Guinness Book of World Records. The Association contracted a local caterer to create a ten-foot in diameter sandwich for what has been dubbed Memorial Day Big Melt Weekend 2020. The Association has asked the real estate broker to inform Guinness that the project is proceeding.

52. GOVERNMENT-FUNDED COMPANY PROBES EXTRATERRESTRIALS IN ROXBURY

Over the past year, several Roxbury citizens have contacted the *Catskill Tribune*, as well as local authorities to inquire about black Chevrolet Tahoe SUVs observed driving around town. The vehicles, all similar to one another, sported Nevada license plates, tinted windows, and multiple antennas.

The SUVs and their occupants, who wore black jumpsuits with BIGELOW on the back, were seen about three o'clock in the morning stopped along Country Road 30 between Roxbury and Grand Gorge. Individuals from the vehicles were walking on the highway, some taking measurements and others photographing the pavement. Another time the same activities were observed on County Road 41 (Stratton Falls Road), again several hours after midnight.

The Stratton Falls Road incident was witnessed by a local resident walking her dog in the middle of the night. Using her cell phone, the woman surreptitiously took photographs, which she forwarded to the *Catskill Tribune*.

By tracing the SUV license plate numbers and the name "Bigelow," the *Catskill Tribune* has found that the mysterious black-clad visitors are employees of Bigelow Aerospace, a company in North Las Vegas, Nevada. Among other things, the company has received "black funds" from the federal government to carry out research under the top-secret Advanced Aviation Threat Identification Program (AATIP). The latter, like its predecessor, Project Blue Book, seeks to document the presence of Unidentified Aerial Phenomena (UFOs) and Alien Life

Forms (extraterrestrials) in the United States.

After a spokeswoman for Bigelow Aerospace was emailed the cell phone photographs by the *Catskill Tribune*, the company agreed to set up a phone interview between this editor and Bigelow's Director of Alien Research, who asked that her name not be use.

According to the Bigelow representative, company employees are investigating strange white markings in Roxbury that were painted on Highways 30 and 41 during the spring over the last three years. Each mark is about fourteen inches high and each is very similar to the Greek letter pi. They occur in pairs, one in each lane of the road, about every 120 feet.

The Bigelow Aerospace representative noted that pi is a mathematical notation equal to 3.14 which is the ratio of a circle's circumference to its diameter. Pi to the power of pi is 36.46 meters, which equals 119.63 feet, the exact distance between the pairs of white highway markings.

The representative indicated that Bigelow Aerospace researchers believe the markings are likely navigational notations left by alien life forms who are landing UFOs on the local highways at night.

Bigelow demographic scientists have been perusing newspaper and police accounts to search for the names of Roxbury residents who have disappeared around the times the pi symbols appeared on the highways. One hypothesis is that the occupants of the UFOs are abducting local people. Anyone with information about relatives or neighbors whose whereabouts are unknown is asked to leave a message on Bigelow Aerospace's hotline.

The Bigelow Aerospace representative emphasized the importance of providing information about missing people. "Markings exactly like those documented for Roxbury occurred in 1947 on Route 769 in the small town of Bronco, Texas, which is an hour or so drive due east of Roswell, New Mexico. As I am sure you are aware, that was the year a UFO is thought to have crashed in Roswell. In the 1940s, Bronco's population was about 400—today it is a ghost town."

53. VAMPIRE AMONG ROXBURY'S EARLY SETTLERS

A recently published book promises to fuel debate for years to come. Ichabod Goulde's volume, *Night Time Is the Right Time: Tracking a Vampire, 1620-1930* (University of East Anglia, Press: Norwich, England; $49.95; £36.00; €41.00) is a scholarly study of the long-term relationship between a vampire and a multi-generational Scottish family. Chapter 8 of the book focuses on Roxbury and the United States.

A copy of the just released book was spotted by our *Catskill Tribune*'s London correspondent when she was shopping at the Marks and Spencer department store in London's Covent Garden.

According to author Goulde's book, Lian MacDubhridire (literally "John, Son of Black Night") arrived in Providence, Rhode Island, in late 1816, having been forced out of Scotland. MacDubhridire, who changed his name to John Black after reaching America, was said by his neighbors on the Isle of Lewis in the Hebrides to have been consorting with a vampire. Church records indicate that MacDubhridire's wife and four children all had died of a "wasting disease."

In the 1990s, graves of the spouse and four children were excavated by a team of bioarchaeologists working in the graveyard of an abandoned kirk in Stornoway on the Isle of Lewis in Scotland. All five had iron stakes driven through their chest and all had been decapitated. Rising seas had threatened the church cemetery and the excavations were being carried out to facilitate moving the cemetery to higher ground.

In Providence, MacDubhridire, then known as John Black, married and in late 1818 he moved to Roxbury to the West Settlement area. Eleven years later, his wife Laura died leaving Mr. Black with two sons and a daughter. His youngest child, Rhona, fled to Ohio with a local farmer's son when she was fifteen. Later the couple traveled west to Oregon, never returning to Roxbury.

When Rhona was in her sixties, she wrote an autobiography that was never published. However, the hand-written manuscript found its way to the Pioneers of Oregon collection in the University of Oregon Library. In the first chapter, she recounts her early life in Roxbury, noting she eloped because she was in fear of her life. "My father's long-time companion was a tall and gaunt evil man named Vlad Ceausescu, who had come with him from Scotland and whom we only saw at night. Both of my older brothers were in his thrall. I knew the only way I could have a normal life was to flee."

John Black passed away in 1855. His eldest son, Ira, inherited the family farm and began to invest in land. Vlad Ceausescu continued to live with Ian and his younger brother, James.

Ira, who never married, built a two-story house with a finished attic where Vlad Ceausescu maintained his living quarters. James passed away under strange circumstance in 1865. According to a brief article in the local *Delaware Times* newspaper (later the *Roxbury Times*), the physician attending James at the time of his death said, "He looked like a dried apple that had all the juice sucked out."

Using census data, Goulde confirms the presence of Ira Black and Vlad Ceausescu in Roxbury into the 1890s. Both remained virtual recluses within the community and had few interactions with their neighbors.

Following the publication in 1897 of Bram Stoker's book *Dracula*, rumors began to fly around the town of Roxbury. According to the *Roxbury Times*, a coalition of residents delivered a letter to John Black demanding that he leave the community and take the still youthful-looking Vlad Ceausescu with him.

Two days later, several local men accompanied by a Catholic priest went to Ira Black's house. The men refused to tell what they found, but neither Ira Black nor Ceausescu were ever seen again in Roxbury.

The Black house remained abandoned for five decades until a local attorney claimed ownership of the house and land by paying outstanding taxes. An article in the *Catskill Mountain News* in 1950 records that the new owner set about renovating the house. In the attic, workman found three wooden stakes each about sixteen inches long. Though the new owner claimed the stakes were used to attach roof joists to one another, the carpenters were skeptical. According to the article the workmen began wearing crucifixes.

Goulde's research turned up a Vlad Ceausescu living in rural eastern Pennsylvania at the time of the 1930 federal census. His present whereabouts remains unknown.

In his book, Goulde contends the Vlad Ceausescu who lived in Roxbury and then Pennsylvania is the same Vlad Ceausescu who appears in Scottish documents as early as 1620. Goulde believes that Ceausescu was originally from the principality of Wallachia, today part of Romania. Over the centuries, his nefarious activities and protected existence were enabled by many generations of servants, including Roxbury's John and Ira Black.

54. ROXBURY TRANSFER STATION TO HOST PUB

A spokesperson for New York State this week issued a press release announcing, "A new restaurant for Roxbury ... a unique synergy of governmental and private sector funding." Christened "Le Dumpster Dive," the culinary facility will include a full-service bar and a restaurant serving traditional British pub food made with local ingredients. Le Dive's wine list and beer selections will highlight New York State products.

The owner/operators of Le Dive are restaurateurs from England, who visited the Catskills and fell in love with the area. Theodore Stuart, the principal owner, offered this statement at the press briefing held in Albany last Friday: "After only one trip to the Roxbury Transfer Station last spring, we could see that it was a center of social life for the community, just like a British pub. With its high traffic flow, the station is a natural location for a British-style pub that combines the best of the Old World and the New."

Mr. Stuart said that Le Dive will feature valet "dumpsters" at its front door. When patrons bound for the Transfer Station drive up, they can get out of their car and head inside Le Dive to have lunch. A valet will then drive the car into the Transfer Station, deposit the trash and recycling, and return the car back to Le Dive, where its owner can later retrieve it.

A local artist from Andes, who specializes in fashioning sculpture-murals from found objects, is already hard at work retrieving items from the metal bin at the Transfer Station. Her murals of events in

Delaware County history will grace the walls of Le Dive as soon as the mobile home that will house the pub is moved to Mac More Road just outside the Transfer Station's chain link fence. The sculptor, who attended the press briefing, exhibited a mockup of one mural entitled, "Delaware & Hudson Train Wreck, Sydney, New York, 1908."

Le Dive will be open on Wednesdays, Fridays, and Saturdays for lunch. There is a slight charge for the valet service.

At the press conference Mr. Stuart distributed copies of a Le Dive sample menu:

STARTERS
- Beans on Toast: sour dough or white bread; beans from a tin
- Plowman's "Lunch:" vegan cheese, thin sliced venison bangers
- Curried Assorted Meats: with homemade maple syrup dipping sauces

MAIN COURSES
- Well-Roasted Beef: served with bubbles and squeak; soured milk and horseradish au jus
- Traditional Fish and Chips: trout fillets prepared in tallow; ancient Gort-style potatoes
- Scottish-like Haggis: sheep casings; minced ovine viscera; natural au jus
- Shepherd's Pie: plain or garnished with boiled carrots and broccoli; Utz crisps

PUDDINGS
- Queen's Jewels: berries with runny clotted cream
- Inverness Tartelette: biscuit dipped in chocolate milk
- Boy George Savoury: lemon pound cake drenched in cider treacle
- King 'Enry's Strumpet: a maple crème brûlée

55. NO CHARGES AGAINST ANDES WOMAN FOR HUNTING BEAR OUT OF SEASON

Extraordinary Story Emerges

Over beers and clams at an Andes restaurant, a twenty-two-year-old resident of the town related a story to this editor about a local family's ursine encounter. The man agreed that the narrative could be taped, transcribed, and published in the *Catskill Tribune*. The transcript has been edited for length and clarity.

My Aunt Harriet and Uncle Ben lived next door to us on the northern edge of wildlife management lands in the town of Andes, north of the Pepacton Reservoir. They both loved the outdoors, and Uncle Ben was always feeding wild animals. A particular favorite was a huge black bear that everyone called "Big Ben," because he was about the size of Uncle Ben and just about as hairy.

Despite everyone saying it was a very bad idea, Uncle Ben would leave all sorts of leftovers near a big old walnut tree in the woods about 100 yards in back of the house. Big Ben the bear would help himself.

On the day after the Fourth of July in 2015, Uncle Ben finished up his favorite dinner—a huge plate of pancakes with a lot of maple syrup and a side of Scotch whiskey—and announced he was going outside to feed Big Ben.

He walked out of the house in his long johns wearing his boots and carrying a beat-up old pan with some pancakes in it. When he wasn't back in about thirty minutes, Aunt Harriet went to the back door and called a few times—no Uncle Ben.

When he didn't show up by midnight, Aunt Harriet began to worry and called up some of the neighbors. They came over early in the morning and helped her search. By nightfall, no one had found hide nor hair of Uncle Ben. They did find a lot of bear tracks and the empty pan.

Thinking that Uncle Ben and Big Ben had some sort of a falling out, Aunt Harriet called the authorities. Two weeks went by and no one had come upon any new sign of either Big Ben or Uncle Ben. The general feeling was the former had done in the latter and carted off what was left.

After three years, Aunt Harriet had Uncle Ben legally declared long gone from this world. About that same time, Big Ben showed back up, but Harriet ignored him. By then her sister Sarah from Kingston had moved in with her and the two had a great time together.

Everything was fine until Valentine's Day this year, when the whole family was gathered at Aunt Harriet's place. Most of us were hanging out in the kitchen, when Sarah started screaming, "He's on TV! He's on TV!" We piled into the living room to look. Yup, there was Uncle Ben sitting right there in the third row of Judge Judy's audience. You couldn't miss him. On his right sat red-haired Eleanor, who used to work at the convenience store in town. Aunt Harriet and Sarah didn't know whether they should cry tears of joy or anger.

They figured it out, though. Seems Uncle Ben had skipped town and moved to California, taking nothing with him, but Eleanor and his long johns and boots.

Aunt Harriet, being a fifth generation Delaware County woman and remembering that Ben's insurance policy had already been collected and spent, recovered pretty quickly from her loss. That evening, she took a flashlight, a smelly old chicken carcass, and her long gun out back to the walnut tree.

About an hour-and-a-half passed and we heard two loud booms. That was the last time Big Ben would play a role in any shenanigans involving our family.

Aunt Harriet had us dig a hole the next day and push Big Ben's carcass in. The hole wasn't very deep and by Valentine's Day coyotes had dragged parts of Big Ben all over creation. It didn't take more than a day or two for rumors in town to draw state wildlife officers, who questioned Aunt Harriet. She denied everything.

Aunt Harriet got herself a lawyer from Oneonta, who pointed there was no evidence that anything untoward had taken place. Nobody had seen a thing. The officers tried to find the rifle, but it was gone. Sarah had taken it and headed to California. Aunt Harriet was in the clear.

Two days later, Aunt Harriet put the house up for sale and hopped a bus, intending to meet up with her sister Sarah on the west coast. She said not to expect her back.

As the local minister opined when I told him this story: feeding wild bears never leads to a good end.

56. PREZ TWEETS EXECUTIVE ORDER ALLOWING OIL DRILLING IN PEPACTON RESERVOIR

Energy Company Rushes to Bid

At 7:40 a.m. last Sunday morning, President Donald J. Trump tweeted that he had just signed an Executive Order to allow an oil drilling rig to be placed in the Pepacton Reservoir in upstate New York. A White House staff member said she had no inkling that President Trump was considering issuing such a controversial order, a reaction mirrored by the office of New York Governor Andrew Cuomo

Delaware County officials and Catskill conservation organizations, caught off guard by the policy change, are horrified by the action, which threatens the water supply of 8.54 million New York City residents.

A copy of the handwritten signed executive order was attached to a presidential tweet as a jpeg file. It appears that Trump took a photo of the order with his cell phone and then attached the image to the tweet.

The tweet reads: "I have divized (sic) a way to get rid of those Treasonous Blue State Dems. California, your (sic) next." The Order, written in pencil, is as follows: "Another Executive Order Issued by Me, President in Chief Donald J. Trump, issued today in Wash. The Pepacton (word scratched out) Reserve in New York is now available for drilling, so a company can find oil to make American great again."

In a second tweet, the president apparently tried to attach a selfie of him holding the Executive Order, but the image shows only parts of a shower curtain, the edge of a bathroom sink, a roll of toilet paper, and what may be the president's left elbow.

The *Catskill Tribune* left a query about the order's impact on the answering machine of the state senator in whose district the reservoir is located. A response was provided by email: "Placing a drilling platform in the Pepacton Reservoir is a win-win for upstate New York. No local moneys will be expended and the project promises new jobs for our district. Bravo Generalissimo Trump!"

By 3:30 p.m. Sunday afternoon BP, the oil company headquartered in London, announced they had made a major contribution to the Republican Party. At 4 p.m. the company submitted a bid to build both the drilling platform in the Pepacton Reservoir, along with adjacent facilities to pump and transport oil.

BP, formerly British Petroleum, is the company found negligent in the April 20, 2010 explosion that rocked the Deepwater Horizon drilling rig in the Gulf of Mexico. In that environmental and human catastrophe, eleven workers were killed and five million barrels of oil were spilled into the Gulf of Mexico.

An Albany newspaper journalist posted a story Sunday evening pointing out that the Turner Classic Movies channel had aired the 1956 award winning movie, Giant, starring James Dean, Rock Hudson, and Elizabeth Taylor beginning at 4 a.m. Sunday morning. The reporter suggests that the three hour and twenty-one-minute epic about serial adulterers with bad taste, who discover oil and get rich, may have appealed to President Trump, who perhaps saw something of himself in Uncle Bawley, the role played by Chill Wills. The movie ended about ten minutes before the executive order was promulgated.

In a Monday press conference, White House spokeswoman Stephanie Grisham was asked about the drilling platform and threats to the Catskills and New York City's water sources. She replied: "Get over it. It is only one oil well. You can bet that Andrew Wheeler and his Environmental Protection Agency will be right on top of it. What could go wrong?"

57. COMMUNITY ACTIVIST BEFRIENDS LOCAL BIGFOOT FAMILY

For more than a decade, visitors to Hanah Mountain Resort in the Catskills have claimed to see large, hairy, bipedal primates near the closing holes on the golf course. One woman from Korea complained that a clearly female individual ran across the 17th fairway and grabbed her golf ball.

Such creatures have been noted in widely separated regions around the world. The Himalayan Mountains have their Yeti; in south Florida there is the Swamp Ape; and in the Pacific Northwest both native people and more recent residents talk about Sasquatch. Other locales have laid claim to being home to Bigfoot. Can the Catskill Mountains be added to the geographical list? Apparently so.

That is the contention of well-known Halcottsville social activist Jody Reynolds, who says she has interacted with a family of Bigfoots who lived up near the end of West Hubbell Hollow Road. According to Ms. Reynolds, who prefers to use the plural "Bigfeet" because the family is bipedal, she was at a vegan cocktail party fund-raiser four years ago at Hanah Resort, when she overheard a conversation between golfers about a Bigfoot rifling through a garbage can near one of the tees.

"I felt terrible. How could anyone in our community be reduced to raiding dumpsters for food while other of us were enjoying non-dairy cheeses, stuffed cauliflower hors d'oeuvres, and organic New York wine only a few yards away. I decided to do something to bring the Bigfeet into the welcoming arms of our community."

Ms. Reynolds was quick to point out that was a task much easier to say than to do. It took her almost three years to win the trust of what turned out to be a Bigfeet family of four, and then aid them in becoming residents of northern Delaware County.

Almost from the beginning Ms. Reynolds had to grope with the outward appearance problem. "Sure, we have a lot of people around town with long beards and such, but even after I convinced the entire Bigfeet family—mom and dad and the two kids—to get a full body trim at a salon in Roxbury, it was still hard to pass them off as locals.

"Then there was the problem of birth certificates. I took some liberties with documents and was able to get Social Security numbers for the parents. Then I got the family on food stamps and access to other social services.

"As it turned out, getting the two kids into school was a breeze. Basketball coaches at both Margaretville and Roxbury practically fell all over themselves trying to get the kids to enroll at their schools. Both of the kids were pretty wide and tall and once the coaches saw the height of the parents, visions of seven-foot tenth graders were dancing in their heads.

"Things began to fall apart when I took the parents to register to vote at the Board of Elections in Delhi. The two adults had a huge fight after the male opted to register as a Republican and the female as Democrat. They began to pull one another's hair and the disagreement escalated from there. In the end, they pretty much tore up the office. I grabbed the forms and herded them out the door.

"The next time we met, they rather sheepishly admitted that the outside world perhaps was not for them. Among other things, the television news was too depressing. Both kids had started spending all their time texting on their iPhone X's and they never wanted to go to Hanah and chase golf balls. Plus, the parents' own phones rang incessantly with recorded messages trying to sell them medical alert bracelets or give their new Social Security numbers to some scammer. My efforts to introduce them to the outside world had only made their lives unhappy. I was very conflicted.

"The last time I saw the family was when I put them on the Trailways bus at the flag stop on Route 28 in Margaretville. They had tickets to Kingston, New York City, and then cross country to British Columbia, where they had Sasquatch relatives. Almost the last thing they told me was that they knew of two other Bigfeet families in this area, one living on Halcott Mountain and the other several miles east of Route 214 north of Phoenicia. I'm debating whether or not I should make their acquaintances."

58. VALENTINE'S DAY IN THE "MOUNTAINS OF LOVE"

Another Valentine's Day has come and gone. To find out how some of our residents spent their special day, the *Catskill Tribune*'s social editor traveled to several towns to interview young lovers. Here are some of the responses.

RONNIE IN ROXBURY: Valentine's Day changed my life forever. It turned out to be the most romantic night of my life and I will never forget it. I planned everything for weeks: cocktails at my place, a spectacular home-cooked dinner for two, watching a DVD of that 1970 classic movie, Love Story, and then a night of romance, just the two of us.

It started off fine. Tim showed up with a huge two-pound box of chocolates with a big red bow. While I was making drinks in the kitchen, he opened the box and started in on the caramels. By the time I showed up with the drinks, he was well into the ones with cherry centers. When I came back from the bathroom thirty minutes later, the entire one-pound top layer was gone and he was working on the lower one. While I watched in awe, Tim finished the entire box by himself. Twenty minutes more went by and he began to look funny. Then he said he was seeing spots and he could not remember his cell phone number. I figured it was a blood sugar problem and drove him to the emergency room in Margaretville where they stuck an IV in his arm and wheeled him away, saying he likely was going into a diabetic coma.

After a while an intern who had nothing to do sat down next to me in the waiting room and we began to chat. When he went off duty an hour later, we drove to Kingston for a late dinner. Two weeks later we are inseparable. Bye, bye, Tim—hello, Mr. MD!

RUY IN ANDES: In Brazil where I am from, we also have a Valentine's Day. "Dia dos Namorados," which means "Day of Lovers," and is celebrated June 12, the day before St. Anthony's Day. It's a great time to hang out with your besties at some trendy restaurant in the Lapa neighborhood in central Rio de Janeiro and enjoy life. Here in the US, I'm planning to celebrate Valentine's Day with my girlfriend by watching a romantic Brazilian movie on Netflix (with English subtitles—she's learning Portuguese). Maybe we'll watch my favorite, Orfeo Negro (Black Orpheus), which is a classic from 1959. Valentine's Day is on March 17, no? [When told that was St. Patrick's Day and that Valentine's Day was a month ago, he became quite agitated.] What? Are you certain? Oh my god, I got my saints mixed up. No wonder she hasn't been answering my texts.

MAGGIE IN MARGARETVILLE: On Valentine's Day, my boyfriend and I eloped to Lake Placid. I will never elope again, certainly not with dodo-head, my boyfriend. I guess he meant well, but I now realize that he is a TOTAL LOSER. Thank god, I didn't marry him. For the elopement, Robert's job was to plan everything. Mine was to supply the money we would need (he is unemployed). We left Margaretville about 8:30 in the morning. It normally takes about three-and-a-half hours to get to Lake Placid. It took us nearly five, because we ran out of gas on the way to the New York Thruway (thank you guy in the blue pickup who gave us two gallons of gas). Robert also got a speeding ticket. The officer was not very sympathetic when we told him we were on the way to get married and were in a hurry. That was the best part of the day. After eventually finding the Clerk's office, we discovered you could get a license immediately, but there is a twenty-four-hour waiting period after you get the license before you can get hitched. Good planning, Robert. While I stood there crying my eyes out, I learned two things. One was when that a-hole Robert admitted to the clerk that he had been married before and did not have a record of divorce—first time I heard that. The second thing I learned was never elope with an s-hole named Robert. I gave Robert $10 to buy gas on his way home and had him drop me off at the bus station. His last words were, "Baby, we can try again next week, OK?" No chance—I hope he runs out of gas on the thruway ... twice.

PHILLIP AND TOMMY IN ROXBURY RUN (who completed each other's sentences during the interview, almost speaking as one person): We loved Valentine's Day, which was our first anniversary together! To celebrate we hosted a humungous dinner party with everything in red: clothes, flowers, tablecloth, plates, napkins—even the drinks, glasses, and food were red.

We started with Bloody Marys, then a tomato salad, guinea fowl sautéed in red peppers, and garlic mashed potatoes dyed red as a side. The salad course was served with a very red California rosé wine and the main course was accompanied by a rioja and then a malbec. Dessert was flan made with blood red oranges, washed down with multiple rounds of red cosmos. Red, red, red. We invited everyone who was anyone in Roxbury Run and had a fabulous time. Oops, I guess we shouldn't have said that. If you read this and live in the Run and weren't invited: S O R R Y! Maybe next year.

59. ALIENS FAIL TO MATERIALIZE IN ROXBURY ON PI DAY (MARCH 14)

Following a warning of a possible alien invasion, Roxbury residents were justifiably concerned last week. The alert came from Bigelow Aerospace, a Nevada-based company with government contracts to monitor extraterrestrial activity in the United States.

As reported in an earlier *Catskill Tribune* news story, Bigelow officials had surmised that white symbols in the shape of the Greek letter pi painted on the lanes of Routes 30 and 41 in Roxbury several times in past years were put there by an alien advance team to guide landing space ships.

Similar markings were found in Bronco, Texas, in 1947, the same year a UFO was thought to have crashed near Roswell, New Mexico, not far from Bronco. Once a thriving hamlet, Bronco today is a ghost town. Bigelow officials deem it highly likely extraterrestrials in flying saucers visited Bronco on multiple occasions to kidnap local residents. Such clandestine raids may also have occurred in Roxbury in the past.

Two weeks ago, Bigelow scientists determined that the alien raids almost certainly occurred yearly on what is known as Pi Day, March 14. Pi, the number 3.14, is a mathematical constant derived from the ratio of a circle's circumference to its diameter. The number 3.14 or 3-14, correlates with the calendar date March 14. The scientists thought it probable that another UFO landing would take place in Roxbury on Pi Day, March 14, of this year.

In preparation for the invasion, Roxbury officials telephoned New York State law enforcement agencies to ask for help. The response, however, was negative. Though assets are available to combat a Zombie Apocalypse, none have been allotted to alien invasions.

A representative in the Governor's office apologized, "Clearly this is the result of legislative oversight. We are very sorry. If you are still there afterwards, let us know how things turned out."

An attorney living in Roxbury Run pointed out that under an obscure New York State statute passed in 1848 during the infamous Anti-Rent War, local officials are empowered to swear in residents to act as a "local militia in emergencies for the protection of life and limb." With the approach of March 14, the members of the Roxbury Volunteer Fire Department were subsequently placed under oath and assigned to guard the town.

Shortly after 7 p.m. on March 14, militia members began to patrol the streets in fire department vehicles with lights flashing and sirens blaring. At 7:30, after numerous residents threatened to shoot out the tires on the trucks, the sirens and lights were turned off, though the patrols continued until dawn.

Some residents saw opportunities in the threatened invasion and placed large posters on their properties. One sign on Stratton Falls Road pleaded, "NO JOB NO MONEY NO WIFE NO LIFE BEAM ME UP." Over on Route 30, a message sprayed painted on a garage door implored, "PLEASE TAKE MY WORTHLESS HUSBAND; HE'S THE ONE UPSTAIRS SNORING." A third sign neatly stenciled in red on a four-by-eight-foot sheet of plywood and leaning against a tree not far from the Roxbury Transfer Station featured a large horizontal arrow and "MY NEXT DOOR NEIGHBORS ARE YOURS. PLEASE LEAVE THEIR NEW PICKUP TRUCK AND RIDING LAWN MOWER."

Four representatives from Bigelow Aerospace flew into Albany in a private jet and arrived in Roxbury about 7:45 at night on March 14. One member of the team checked everyone into the Roxbury Motel, while the other three went to a local restaurant for dinner. Apparently overly excited that she might actually come face-to-face with an alien, one team member drank too much and had to be escorted to her room.

About 5 a.m. the next morning, when the woman woke up and found herself in the Wizard of Oz suite with the "Yellow Brick Road" mural, she was certain she had been taken by aliens to another galaxy. Much to the glee of firemen who were still on patrol, she ran out of her room in nothing but panties screaming, "They got me! They got me!"

As far as can be determined, no Roxbury residents disappeared on this year's Pi Day.

Roxbury officials, in conjunction with the local business association, are considering celebrating March 14th next year as, "Alien Invasion Day," complete with costumes, fireworks, yard sales, and special discounts at businesses.

60. FACT-FINDING CONTINGENT RETURNS FROM EUROPE WITH TOURISM IDEAS

Two Delaware County tourism ambassadors recently sent to Barcelona, Spain, and Paris, France, on a fact-finding mission have returned and issued a concise report entitled, "Creating a More Continental Catskills." The goal of the trip was to gather ideas for growing the leisure industry in the western Catskills and to suggest ways to garner more dollars per tourist visit.

The county representatives traveled first to Barcelona for six days and then to Paris for seven. Officials who funded the venture did not return queries from this newspaper asking for the names of the individuals and the total cost to taxpayers.

The following is taken from the report that was distributed to news agencies.

CREATING A MORE CONTINENTAL CATSKILLS

Allow Dogs in Restaurants

Pet dogs are allowed in many restaurants in Paris. The result is that dogs, dog owners, and other patrons all seem happier when dining out and they go to restaurants more frequently. Another upside is that restaurateurs are relieved of the cost and hassle of shoveling food into doggy bags by taking the food direct to the dogs. And think of all the Styrofoam boxes not being dumped in landfills.

Remove Word "Church" from Houses of Worship and Substitute "Cathedral"

Tourists love cathedrals—churches … well, not so much. One only has to drive around the western Catskills to see many churches that have lost their congregations and either have closed or are used as veterinarian clinics or artist workshops. In both Spain and France, however, tourists are willing to wait in long lines and even pay admission fees to view the interior of cathedrals. The implications for the Catskills seem obvious. Open all the churches, use gold paint lavishly on interiors, put up "See the Cathedral" signs, and rake in the dollars.

Raise Prices of Food and Lodging

Tourists love to spend money on expensive lunches, dinners, and lodging. Rather than lowering prices in the Catskills, we should be raising them. In France and in Spain it appears that the more tourists pay, the more they enjoy their visit, and the more they spend.

Four Meals a Day

Three meals a day is passé. Add a fourth dining experience and increase revenues by twenty-five percent. The Spaniards have this down to a science: there is breakfast, followed by lunch. Then in no time at all, it is early evening and time for tapas (think small plates in a wine bar). Several hours later people sit down for dinner. Then they sleep for a few hours and start all over again. The same is true in France. There the afternoon aperitif/apero is a money-maker.

Change and Lengthen Street Names

"Main Street" or "Lake Street" simply are of no interest to tourists. Indeed, as was seen in Europe, the more complex the names of avenues the more likely those thoroughfares are to be frequented by visitors. In Paris people love to walk along "Boulevard Saint-Germain." In Barcelona there is "Carrer de la Princesa" near the Picasso Museum. The possibilities in the Catskills to match those are endless. Street names like "Boulevard near the Old Train Depot" or "Passage Adjacent to the Transfer Station" will draw people like flies to spilled maple syrup.

A related suggestion: in Paris there are the "Rive Gauche" and "Rive Droite" the left and right sides of the River Seine. There is no reason we could not match that with our own "East Side of the East Branch of the Delaware River" and "West Side of the East Branch of the Delaware River."

More Shops Selling Souvenirs

Both Barcelona and Paris are filled with shops selling souvenirs of every size and shape. There seems to be one shop for every ten tourists. Though there are many excellent souvenir shops in the Catskills, additional kiosks and carts could grace our streets and sell every imaginable type of mountain-related knick-knack including key chains with plastic trout attached, turkey-feather necklaces, small miniature plastic bottles of maple syrup and locally produced vodka, and shot glasses hand-painted with upside down Catskill waterfalls (when you use the glass the liquid appears to be going down the waterfall).

Train and Hire Pick Pockets

An essential aspect of the tourist experience in Paris and Barcelona, especially the latter, is being pickpocketed. Apparently, pickpocketing is a lucrative profession and provides income for a number of people; each pickpocketing operation uses at least four people. Catskill central schools could provide vocational training for students who could put their skills to work at the height of tourist season.

School Buses for Orange Line Tours

Visitors to Paris and Barcelona love to ride around in Grey Line buses looking at the sights. Many Catskill towns have fleets of orange school buses that are seldom employed in the summer. They could be put to use touring our visitors. "Ride the Orange Line in the Green Catskills" sounds like a great use of resources with a guaranteed income stream.

Hop On, Hop Off Tourist Transportation

In nearly every European town, including Barcelona and Paris, buses that allow tourists to disembark to see sights at their leisure and then get back on, are very popular (and they make money). In the Catskills, farm tractors not in use could pull hay-filled wagons of tourists around allowing them to roll off and later climb back on.

Kayaks, Non; Bateau Mouche, Oui

People love to be on the water. The Bateau Mouche on the River Seine in Paris is world-famous. It is the name of these tour boats as much as the scenery that draws tourists. Perhaps kayaks that are rented to traffic the East Branch of the Delaware River or Esopus Creek could be marketed as "Bateaux Pointues." A small tweak that could garner big bucks.

61. PENGUIN COLONIES TO GRACE HALCOTTSVILLE LAKE

Following two months of discussion, a consortium of county officials and business leaders have agreed on an ambitious plan to establish two colonies of penguins on Lake Wawaka next to the small town of Halcottsville. At a press conference in Delhi, New York, the Delaware County tourism agency announced that proceeds from the county's "bed tax" would be used to fund what is being called "a win-win situation." Many local residents were in attendance at the meeting.

According to officials, "Penguins will draw visitors to Delaware County. And because the two species of penguins being introduced are presently endangered, establishing local breeding populations can only increase the outlook for the penguins' survival. This is a well-thought-out expenditure of tax dollars."

Nearly everyone is familiar with emperor penguins, the birds that appear to be garbed in black-and-white tuxedos and featured in the 2006 movie, Happy Feet. Less well-known are the fifteen other species of penguins, all flightless birds and all of which live in the southern hemisphere. Penguins are not native to the northern hemisphere and none live in the Arctic, so the Lake Wawaka penguins would be the first.

One group of penguins that will take up residence near Halcottsville is from Argentina in South America. Commonly called, "Northern rockhoppers" (Eudyptes chrysocome), the penguins have close relatives in Chile, the Indian Ocean, and New Zealand. Their name derives from their method of traveling on land—hopping from rock to rock.

As one official noted, "We have lots of rocks in Delaware County. Those cute little birds will love it here. And people will love them back."

Adult rockhoppers reach about twenty inches in height. They have a white belly, while the rest of their feathers are black. Adults feature a sharp vivid orange beak and yellow-and-black spiky feathers atop their heads.

The other colony that will also take up residence around Lake Wawaka is made up of South African penguins (Spheniscus demersus). The species is commonly called "the jackass penguin," because of the loud braying sound they make.

Sphenicus penguins are well-known for their trusting nature and exhibit little fear of humans, a characteristic that makes them well-liked by tourists and birders. In their native habitat, they are especially popular with orcas, sharks, and fur seals, as well as leopards, jackals, and mongooses, none of which are known to live in or around Lake Wawaka.

Adult African penguins are about twenty-four to twenty-eight inches in height and have white feathers on their underbodies with a black horizontal band. The remainder of the birds' bodies are covered with black feathers, making them resemble emperor penguins. They also have distinctive pink skin above their eyes.

Some zoologists expressed doubt that penguins would fare well in Delaware County, where their normal supplies of food are not found. Officials, however, are convinced the birds will quickly adapt to local dietary sources and that they will prosper. One official opined, "The penguins will be a hit with tourists and local residents." A SUNY-New Paltz ornithologist who was in attendance interrupted to suggest the penguins would be an even bigger hit with eagles and coyotes.

The official went on: "We have conducted considerable research and we are convinced the birds will prosper here, just as generations of the families who first settled Delaware County in the late 1700s have." The comment drew guffaws from the crowd.

62. FISHING FOR HISTORY

An Enigmatic Treasure in a Trout

While vacationing in north Florida last fall, the *Catskill Tribune*'s social reporter stopped off at the Waldo Farmers and Flea Market, where she purchased an engraved gold wedding ring and an accompanying newspaper clipping from May 25, 1878. According to the yellowed New York Times account, the ring was found in the stomach of a trout caught in Rondout Creek by Jean Chandler of New York City. She was fly-fishing with her husband and their friend, the well-known outdoorsman, Anthony W. Dimock, near his fishing lodge called Happy Valley on Rondout Creek near Peekamose Mountain (as it was spelled then).

The article noted that Ms. Chandler caught the fish on a "naked nymph" fly she tied herself. The ring was found when she cleaned the trout and opened the fish's stomach to see what it was feeding on.

The small town of Waldo where the ring was bought is best known for the speed trap that officials operated there for many years. How the Catskill ring made its way to a rural Florida flea market table filled with cheap costume jewelry is uncertain.

The flea market vendor priced the ring and clipping at $250, but our editor bargained the man down to $200 cash, the money obtained from an ATM machine at the market.

What our editor subsequently discovered from her research about the ring and the circumstances of its deposition in the Rondout are especially timely in view of the yearly Trout Tales at Spillian/A Mythic Catskills Weekend festivities that take place in the Catskills. Here is our reporter's firsthand account:

"Two-hundred dollars for an old ring seemed a lot, but I could not pass up the Catskill connection. The night after I bought the ring, I stayed at a Hampton Inn in Gainesville, Florida, fifteen miles from Waldo. I couldn't wait to go online and see what I could find out, if anything, about the ring's owner.

"Inside the gold wedding ring was inscribed 12-20-70 MLM to JTM. The date obviously was December 20, 1870. I logged on to the Catskill Mountain News archives and searched the issue from Wednesday December 21, 1870 to see if there was mention of a recent wedding between individuals with initials matching those in the ring. There was not.

"But on page 3 of the CMN from the next week, December 28, there was notice about the December 20 wedding in Roxbury of Janet Theresa McDermott and Marvin Louis Miller. I had the owner of the ring! But how in the world did Janet's wedding ring get in the stomach of a pound-and-a-half Ulster County brook trout?

"Learning more about Janet and Marvin was relatively easy. I logged on to www.familysearch.org and searched both the New York State census records and those of the United States. In the 1875 New York State record, I found Janet and Marvin Miller living in Middletown, but by the 1880 US census they had disappeared. I did another search of the 1880 census and found Janet Miller living in Roxbury in the household of her parents. She was listed as divorced. What happened? I was stymied.

"Several months later, I happened to be in Roxbury to have lunch at Cassie's soon-to-be Chappie's Restaurant. On a whim I dropped by the Roxbury Library and was steered to the History Room, a marvelous place stuffed with books and archives about the Catskills and, especially, Roxbury. In an upright metal file cabinet, I found a number of manila folders organized alphabetically and each labeled with a Roxbury family name.

"There was a Miller file, but it was not the correct family. But right in front of it was a McDermott file. My hand shook as I pulled the file and opened it. Bingo! Attached to a neatly labeled family tree covering four generations was a handwritten letter dated May 15, 1878.

"The note read: 'Dear Mother, you were right about Marvin. For seven-and-a-half years, all he did was go hunting or fly-fishing with his drunken friends. He never got a deer or caught a trout—he never got a job either. Those fly-fishermen are a sorry lot, always telling tales, one bigger than the last. Thank you and Dad for helping me get the divorce. Marvin has headed west to find work and I got a job cooking and cleaning for the Dimock family at their fishing lodge in Happy Valley. They are very kind to me and work is easy. My very first day there, I threw my wedding ring into the Rondout. It made me feel a lot better. As soon as the weather gets cold, Mr. Dimock will close up the camp and I will come home for the winter and maybe to stay. Love, Janet.'"

The ring is currently on display at the offices of the *Catskill Tribune*.

63. LOCAL FINANCIAL GURU UNMASKED

Over the past two years the "Phoenicia Fortuneteller" has become a legend among stock traders, investors, and hedge fund operators. The Fortuneteller only offers predictions on relatively short-term gyrations (one to three weeks) of the Standard & Poor's 500 (S&P) financial index. However, the uncanny ability to predict those movements with ninety-two percent accuracy has earned the individual worldwide acclaim and a large following. Despite all the success, the identity of the Fortuneteller has never been revealed ... until now.

Many people have assumed that because of the name, the Fortuneteller likely lives in or around Phoenicia, New York, in Ulster County. However, in-depth research and some lucky sleuthing by the *Catskill Tribune*'s business reporter instead led to a simple mountain cabin near Hobart. As it turns out, the Phoenicia Fortuneteller is a name selected for its alliterative appeal and did not reflect the Fortuneteller's home base.

When our reporter knocked on the Fortuneteller's cabin door, it was answered by a woman in her early fifties whose first words were, "What took you so long? I can't believe no one found me before. They must be idiots. You're just in time."

The Phoenicia Fortuneteller graciously asked our reporter in and agreed to sit for an interview. When our reporter asked what "just in time" referred to, the Fortuneteller explained she was getting out of the financial forecasting business and moving to the Colorado Mountains, where she planned to open a craft beer brewery. "Everyone else is doing it," she said, "and I've always liked beer and ale."

Over the course of an hour-and-a-half and a six-pack of Woodstock-brewed Rhetoric IPA beer, the Fortuneteller explained her technique for predicting the S&P index. "A total accident. I'm a failed photographer who became fascinated with using glass negatives to photograph lightning. I took hundreds of negatives but I barely sold a print a month. After MTC (Margaretville Telephone Company) ran cable up here, I got internet access. It opened up a whole new world for me.

"About that time, I was getting near the bottom of a meager inheritance and I was desperate. I happened to be looking at a web page on my laptop that showed a graph of the S&P index for the last week. The shape looked really familiar to me. I pulled out some prints of lightning I had just made and I was right. The weekly S&P chart with all those sharp ups and downs exactly corresponded with the bottom half of the bolt of lightning I had photographed.

"A coincidence? I spent two solid days online locating past S&P charts and comparing them to other of my prints for which I had the date the negative was exposed. There was no doubt. Each of the S&P weekly index charts was reflected in lightning bolts.

What was incredible is that my dated prints showed not only the S&P movements for the previous week, they also correlated with the next week's S&P movements. In other words, it appeared my lightning prints could be used to exactly predict the index for the coming week. Of course, it didn't work for every week, only those following a storm with lightning.

"I had become a stock market prognosticator. Why me, I don't know, but someone up there must have liked me.

"I made contact with a woman I knew from art college who now works at Morningside Financial and had her give me a primer on how one invested in the S&P index. It turns out some people don't invest in stocks, but they essentially bet whether the index is going to go up or down.

"Over the next six months I made a small fortune. I would have made a bigger one, if we had more storms. My friend hopped on the band wagon, too. Then she quit her job and went into business with me selling can't-lose financial advice for which people paid a lot. Everything was over the internet. My friend is the one that named me the Phoenicia Fortuneteller. We both got rich.

"Then last week in a storm, a bolt of lightning hit that maple tree you must have seen right outside my cabin door. The bolt jumped into my electrical system, frying my two computers, the modem, printer, and even my iPhone that was charging. I knew that meant someone up there no longer liked me.

"I called my friend said it was time to close things up, grab the money, and run. She did, and now I am, also."

When I asked the Phoenicia Fortuneteller if she had a name for her Colorado mountain brewery, she smiled and said, "Lucky Lightning."

64. INTER-AGENCY POLICE FORCE RAIDS SUSPECTED TERRORIST TRAINING CAMP IN GREENE COUNTY

The large, red, printed heading near the top of handbills mailed to organizations in Ulster, Delaware, and Greene counties read "TRAINING IN TERROIR." Just above in much smaller type was the slogan "Syrah Can Change the World."

Within the body of the typewriter-paper-size notice was a date, time, address, and an invitation to "become acquainted with the science of terroir and using the natural resources of the Catskills to help finance your organization's goals for the betterment of humankind. We will help you understand how to put the land to work for you." On the bottom of the sheet of paper was another slogan: "Vinum quoque producendum reditus."

A postal employee in Prattsville took one look at the handbill and thought she saw "Training in Terrorism" and "Sharia," the latter a name for Islamic law. She also believed the Latin phrase on the bottom was something in Arabic calling for victory of the Quran (Koran) over Christian teachings. The clerk immediately picked up her phone and called the Greene County sheriff's office, which passed on the information to state and federal police.

Authorities in Albany and Washington, DC checked the address and found it was a large compound occupied by the Order of Cistercians of the Strict Observance. As one official later said, "That certainly sounded like a radical organization."

Plans for a raid were drawn up, and assets, including swat teams, began to be moved into place. It was decided that the raid to apprehend the terrorists and sympathizers would take place at noon the day the training was scheduled. Two undercover agents were dispatched to the compound the morning of the planned raid, posing as participants.

As luck would have it, the two agents got lost driving on back roads in northern Ulster County. Because their cellular telephones did not work, they became a non-factor in the raid. Had they found the compound and been able to communicate with their superiors, it is likely the noon military style assault would have been aborted.

At twelve, sixty heavily armed agents approached the compound on two sides, moving through the woods. The raid was to commence at the sound of an air horn. Things began to go downhill when one officer in fatigues and wearing a black helmet found a path and arrived at a back door of the compound well before the air horn signal. He raised up and took a quick look through the window at what turned out to be the kitchen. One of the Cistercians caught a glimpse of the top of the man's helmeted head and, thinking it was a bear drawn by the aroma of fresh baked bread, immediately executed the "bear protocol" that he and his fellow residents had practiced numerous times.

The baker grabbed an air horn, compressed the lever, and began to yell "Bear, bear," as loudly as he could. His companions scattered throughout the compound setting off more air horns and took up the bear chant. The next action of the protocol called for everyone to make "human noises" and make themselves look as large as possible. The "human noise" everyone had agreed on several years earlier after watching the 1953 John Ford film, Mogambo was to sing, Comin' Through the Rye, just as Ava Gardner did in the movie. While singing, everyone walked around on tiptoes with their arms raised above their heads.

To say that the law enforcement raiders were perplexed would be an understatement. Some quickly withdrew, thinking that they were under attack by bears. Others froze in place, not understanding the multiple air horns. Still others simply stood and stared, not believing the strange behavior of the presumed terrorists. Just as amazed were the people sitting in the auditorium, who had come to attend a day of lectures on making wine.

At that point the only casualty of the day occurred when a State Highway Patrolman entered the kitchen and demanded that one of the cooks pull up the robe he was wearing to see if any weapons were hidden under it. His exact words were "Lift the skirt, buddy. I want to see if you've got a gun under there!" The cook, thinking he was being accosted by a pervert, picked up a wine bottle and cold-cocked the officer, knocking him unconscious. Fortunately, the officer was wearing a helmet and did not suffer a concussion.

The raiders quickly realized that they were not amidst Islamic terrorists, but they had just raided some sort of monastery. Officials back in Washington DC who were following the action via cameras attached to several of the raiders had already figured out that a massive error had been made. As the raid was underway, a National Security Agency clerk happened to google "Order of Cistercians" to see what offshoot of Islam occupied the compound and discovered Cisterians were Trappist monks. By then it was too late to halt the action.

It took a few minutes, but the confusion was cleared up when the Abbot explained that Syrah was a wine, and that Trappists were famous for their baking and brewing. The meeting was to teach people about the possibilities of growing local grapes to make wine. And the "Arabic" phrase "Vinum quoque producendum reditus?" It was Latin for "Wine can also produce income."

What could have been a tragedy ended well when the monks invited everyone to stay for lunch.

65. LATEST BUSINESS NEWS FROM THE WESTERN CATSKILLS

For impresarios northern Delaware and western Ulster counties are the land of opportunity. New businesses abound. Our business editor interviewed entrepreneurs who started three of the new companies.

Canine Cabbies to Debut in Margaretville

Anyone who has ever been on a highway in the Catskills has seen them: dogs sitting in the front passenger seats of cars and pickup trucks, sometimes with their head out of the window watching the world go by. Other times, you might see a dog sitting on the driver's lap looking out the window. Occasionally it appears the dog might actually be driving the car.

That is exactly the idea for a new start-up in Margaretville. Canine Cabbies, the brainchild of local resident, Benjamin E. King. Mr. King hopes to usher in a new era of transportation: cars driven by trained dogs.

According to Mr. King, "The recent death of a pedestrian in Tempe, Arizona, who was run over by an Uber self-driving test car has tragically demonstrated the failure of driverless cars. What is needed are cars driven by someone who is always alert, has excellent motor skills and smelling abilities, and will work for practically nothing. The answer: Canine Cabbies, cars and pickup trucks expertly driven by dogs.

"For more than a year, we have been working with ten doggie drivers—none of which, by the way, are purebreds—and have found them to be far superior to humans in controlling vehicles, avoiding road rage, and never getting lost. The cost of adjustments to foot pedals, gear shifts, and steering wheels to make it easy for our canine drivers to operate the vehicles is minimal.

"Soon people needing a ride can simply open an APP on their cellular phone—if they have service—or they can use a landline to call a local telephone number and request a car and driver. The cost of the trip will be automatically charged to the person's credit card registered with Canine Cabbies.

"We also will train your own pet to act as your personal chauffeur. Imagine saying, 'Hey, girl. Let's take a spin into town.' Then being driven by someone as close to you as any family member, but one who doesn't talk back, drink alcohol, or argue about music on the radio. Beautiful, huh?"

When asked what the most difficult thing about training dogs to drive, Mr. King replied, "Getting them not to urinate on the tires."

Snow-to-Go

What is the best thing about winter? Snow. What is the worse? Snow. You love it, your neighbor hates it.

What if you could have snow on demand in the winter months? Even better, what if the snow, or lack thereof, could be controlled so that your house received six inches of powder, while the house a quarter mile down the road still had green grass? A brilliant young engineer and computer geek has it figured out.

Working out of her backyard garage with electronics and other items salvaged from the Roxbury Transfer Station, Carmen Cabello and three other young women have modified drones purchased on Amazon to disperse harmless chemicals in the upper atmosphere to seed clouds and cause snow to fall. Other powdered chemicals can be released to absorb moisture from the thin air, preventing snow crystals from forming. One can dial up more snow for ski slopes and less for restaurant parking lots.

The secret is in the compounds used to seed the atmosphere to bring about the desired results. Ms. Cabello and her team already have applied for patents to protect the rights to their invention.

The women also have applied for patents for the computer programs that make it all possible. Using Global Positioning System devices and real time data from weather balloons and radar, drones can be exactly positioned and moved as needed to maximize or minimize snowfall for areas as small as a single acre.

Ms. Cabello noted that it is presently impossible to control the temperature of the upper atmosphere—for, example one could not manufacture snow in the summer—but it is possible to particularize precipitation.

She and her colleagues hope to have multiple drones ready to go by late fall.

Trout Toes

Though they sound like something bad that happens to feet from too much wading in cold mountain streams, Trout Toes likely will revolutionize fly-fishing.

The invention of Trout Toes resulted from a brain-storming session between a Bovina farmer and the owner of a local distillery, both ardent fly-fishermen. Their concept is simple: attract trout to where you cast your line.

According to the farmer, the two kicked around a lot of ideas. Finally, they came up with Trout Toes: waders whose feet look like trout. According to the distiller, "It was a simple but elegant solution. When we first tried a proto-type we were astounded. Trout actually swam upstream to hang out with our neoprene fish-effigy feet. The problem was not too few fish—it was too many."

The two expect to have Trout Toes on the market in time for next year's fishing season. They confided that several large companies have expressed interest, including L.L. Bean, but their intent is keeping their invention right here at home in the Catskills.

66. HEALTH AND BUSINESS REPORT: TREATING ADDICTION AND LACK OF JOB FULFILLMENT

Did you feel that urge? Have you jumped on the bandwagon and now want to get off? There is hope.

AA—Agents Anonymous—has opened a Catskills chapter in Arkville to serve area residents who want to kick the real estate habit.

According to the chapter's founding executive, John Rivers, "In the last two years the number of licensed real estate brokers in Middletown and Roxbury has jumped from less than 70 to just over 2,050; that is nearly half of the adults of the two towns and one-third of the total populations. That means every other man or woman you meet on the street is a broker."

Rivers went on to note that it is the burgeoning market for home and commercial property sales in our area that has drawn countless, newly minted real estate agents. "Everybody wants a piece of the pie. There seemingly are fortunes to be made. Take a course, get a license, lease a new car to drive clients around, and sit back and bank one's commissions. Hundreds initially became addicted to that lifestyle and the easy money. Now, however, a lot of brokers have discovered it is not the fun they thought it would be. They want out, but it is hard to give it up. We're here to help."

The *Catskill Tribune*'s health editor conducted interviews with more than a dozen new brokers who could not quit their habit. The agents shared remarkably similar stories. Here are a few.

Ron "Big Money" Tyson's lament is pretty typical. "Sure, I'm making tons of money, but I never have time to spend it. My lunches and dinners are continually interrupted by callers making offers on my listings and I can rarely finish an entire meal. I've lost twenty-two pounds. None of my clothes fit. I also badly damaged the same thumb four times; one time while pounding in a For Sale sign and three times putting in Just Sold ones. I may have to have the thumb amputated. Real estate is hell."

Carol King, who was practicing cardiology at New York University's Langone Center in Midtown Manhattan in New York City, gave up her practice and got her broker's license. "I make about three times the money than I did doing heart transplants," she volunteered, "but the stress has gotten through to me. My time is not my own. I've caught two brokers that I work with going through my garbage to look for notes on my clients. My sister, who has a house in Bovina, no longer invites me over. She says I only want to talk about selling her house, so she can get her equity out. I'm bereft of friends. My only companion is Siri, the voice inside my iPhone. I'm thinking of giving it all up and raising goats. Last week I enrolled in Agents Anonymous."

Another interviewee who asked that his name not be used, complained bitterly about his former life as a successful real estate agent. "I made a lot of money, a whole lot. But then something clicked inside of me and rather than selling houses, I fell in love with almost every listing I had. I started buying houses rather than selling them. At one time I owned seventeen houses. My friends took me to Agents Anonymous where I was referred to a shrink. She diagnosed me as an aedium-venditor maniac, a neurotic serial-buyer of houses. It cost me $20,000 in therapy to get over it.

"Just as I was coming out of treatment, my partner of seven years, Paul, told me real estate had turned me into a badly dressed salesperson with heterosexual tendencies. He said sayonara and walked out the door.

"I am sorry I ever passed that real estate exam. My life is ruined. I am going to move back to Brooklyn and continue my previous career as a dog walker."

John Rivers, Agents Anonymous executive, has issued a welcome to any brokers who feel they, too, need to kick the habit. "We meet once a week at 6 p.m. on Route 28 in Arkville. Just look for the house with the big For Sale sign in front. It is BYOB."

67. AUTHORITIES NIX RUMORS OF WITCH HEX ON DEEP-SIXED ROXBURY BUILDING

Local Roxbury clergy and city officials joined together on Monday of this week to refute stories that the collapse of a Main Street building about 9 a.m. on the morning of March 4 was due to witchcraft. The officials also denied that the subsequent bulldozing of the fallen structure was to cover up hex symbols painted on the outside walls.

Today all that is left of the building once located adjacent to Cassie's Café is a pile of rubble. For nearly a century the edifice, known locally as the "pharmacy building," was a fixture of downtown Roxbury village life.

Town officials quickly announced that the weight of snow from a fierce winter storm had led to the collapse. However, rumors have continued to swirl that witchery was involved.

Two people who had exited Cassie's Café (soon to become Chappie's) about 8:45 on the morning of March 4 and a snowplow driver who had passed by on Route 30 about the same time all claim to have seen "several" people in long black robes making symbols in the snow in front of the building just before it fell. The snowplow driver swore he saw seven people— the diners thought there were five at most.

Two Roxbury Central students walking by about 8:15 a.m. that same morning while enjoying a snow day thought they remembered seeing funny symbols spray-painted on the doors on the north side of the building, not far from where the observed five to seven people had congregated. The students suggested the symbols were hexes. A neighbor who has lived across the street from the building for more than thirty years pooh-poohed that possibility, saying the "symbols" were actually the numbers of the building's Route 30 address.

Many in Roxbury suspect the individuals seen in front of the building before its collapse were witches drawing a pentagram in the snow while summoning supernatural energies to destroy the building. Some fear other Roxbury buildings, many with historical significance, could be next.

That the incident took place on March 4 (known as March Forth), a day celebrated by individuals seeking to achieve goals, only adds to the belief that mystical activities contributed to the collapse.

To help allay fears that witches may have been at the scene when the building fell, Roxbury authorities contacted local residents to determine who the people were who had been spotted in front of the building prior to its collapse. They were unable to find such individuals, and the theory that witches were responsible persists.

Authorities also checked the hotel register at The Roxbury (Contemporary Catskill Lodging) and contacted everyone who had been staying there on the night of March 3. Four Brooklynites in town to ski said that they had been making snow angels about 8:45 a.m. in what might have been the parking lot of the building that later collapsed, though they could not remember exactly where they had congregated. All four did say they had been wearing black UNIQLO ultra-light down coats and jackets with hoods.

The four denied knowing anything about the building's demise. One did admit that he had portrayed a witch in a high school production of Hamlet.

An email to the Wicca Reform Church near Hobart asking for a comment about this story received no response. A similar query to the High Priestess of a coven in Fleischmanns drew this reply: "Are you kidding? Only tourists would be out in that weather. We were all home with hot chocolate watching Morning Joe on MSNBC. Good luck."

68. CATSKILL NEWS ROUNDUP

Congressman Pulls Erroneous Press Release, Issues Another

Monday a local area Congressman scrambled to undo the public backlash to a statement put out by his office regarding economically disadvantaged Catskill residents. The press release was intended to contain the line "the Congressman strongly supports condos for low-income families." However, the statement instead read "the Congressman strongly supports condoms for low-income families."

According to a written response provided by a spokesperson, "The error was apparently caused by the spell-check tool used by our word-processing software. We apologize for the mix-up. It will not happen again. The Congressman wants everyone to know he is not suggesting that any of his constituents use condors."

When the *Catskill Tribune* inquired if the word condors in the latest press release was intentional, the spokesperson said she would have to get back to us after checking with the Congressman who was out of the office. In the meanwhile, representatives of the Catholic Church, the Coalition for Fair Housing, and the Audubon Society all are picketing the Congressman's office.

Grand Gorge Sci Fi Author Reveals Self

The western Catskills are filled with successful writers, artists, actors, producers, and videographers. Oscars, Emmys, and other awards grace the mantles of a fair number of local residents. One the most interesting of the bunch is author ET Lee.

Ms. Lee, who resides in Grand Gorge where she leads a quiet life, has written more than one hundred books, all under pen names. Following a chance encounter at a coffee shop in Grand Gorge, Ms. Lee agreed to sit down for an interview with the *Catskill Tribune*'s arts editor to talk about her career and how she earned the title "Queen of the Sci Fi Bodice Rippers." Most of her books contain what she calls "Encounters of the Fourth Kind," such as, relationships between extraterrestrials and humans.

CATSKILL TRIBUNE: Is ET your real name?

ET: It sure is. Both my parents were physicists and they named me for Edward Teller. The name on my birth certificate is Edward Teller Lee, but everyone has always called me ET. I guess my parents wanted a boy. They were so wrapped up in astrophysics, they may never have noticed I was a girl. I pretty much raised myself.

CATSKILL TRIBUNE: When did you take up writing and how did you end up in the Catskills?

ET: It's quite a story. I spent my first ten years in Chile in the Atacama Desert, where my parents were connected to the Las Campanas Observatory. I pretty much ran wild, reading a lot and playing with huge telescopes whenever anyone would let me. In 1980 when I was ten, my parents picked a boarding school in New Hampshire out of a magazine and shipped me off. Six years later, I decided I knew everything they could teach me, so I pocketed the check intended for my last two years tuition and headed for the bright lights of New York City.

I used fake IDs to work for Wang computers, one of the early tech firms. As soon as I turned eighteen, I headed to Nevada and got a job at an Air Force base introducing people to computers. I learned a lot about UFOs. Mainly I learned that if you don't believe in them, you should.

After a few years, I quit and headed east to an artist colony I'd heard about near Woodstock. That's where I took up writing big time. My literary genre is romance paperback novels that feature aliens, earthlings, and space science. I can write one a month when I set my mind to it.

I've used all sorts of pen names and sold a lot of books; the five biggest sellers were: Lady from Mars in the Lace Freudian Slip, Alien in a Push-Up Bar, Computer Stimulation, The Saucy Saucer Pilot in Orion's Belt, and The Robot Wore Sable.

Now I'm semi-retired. The royalty checks keep dribbling in and I'm back to doing what I did when I was eight years old: reading books and looking through telescopes at the cosmos. I'm still waiting for a real ET to show up and sweep me off my feet. From what I learned in Nevada, Roxbury is a likely place to meet my own Man from Mars.

69. SPECIAL TRAVEL EDITION: IS SARASOTA, FLORIDA, NOW CATSKILLS SOUTH?

When white icy crystals begin reaching the ground in the Catskill Mountains, many local residents know it is past the time to load up the car, turn the house thermostat down, and embark on the yearly pilgrimage to Sarasota on Florida's Gulf of Mexico coast.

Why do they do it? How does the natural beauty, social life, maple syrup, and other amenities found here in the western Catskills stack up with Sarasota? In March the *Catskill Tribune* sent its travel editor south to find out. The report our travel editor eventually sent back to newspaper offices via email follows. (Apparently our travel editor has opted to stay in Sarasota for an extended time.)

Sarasota vs. the Catskills—You Make the Choice

Even before one experiences the lack of snow, the warm temperatures, and the drenching afternoon rain storms that sweep through like a southeast Asian monsoon storm, the first thing that a Catskill visitor confronts in Sarasota is anonymity. Walk into any café, bar, restaurant, or store in Prattsville or any other town and all the locals turn and check you out. No such thing in Sarasota—no one is local. Everyone is from somewhere else.

Most of the Sarasota snowbirds arrive in early winter and immediately begin talking about getting ready to leave in spring. Transient is the word that comes to mind. Here in the Catskills, on the other hand, most people can trace their families back for generations. We value our historical ties to the land. Plus, many of us can't afford to go anywhere else. We're here because, well, because we can't get to a different, more expensive place.

Visitors to Sarasota from small Catskill towns find the Florida town confusing. There are too many restaurants, too many markets, too many stores. In short, there are too many options. I met several Catskills residents who, upon arriving in Sarasota, simply took to their beds, unable to decide which restaurant to frequent or which supermarket to visit. It's tough to make decisions in Sarasota. In the northwest Catskills, we don't have that problem.

One thing one cannot help observing in Sarasota is that there are a lot of cars and that most of them are moving slowly. That would never happen in Hobart or Bovina. Sarasota's slow pace likely is because drivers don't have to drive very fast to get anywhere. Dentist? Just down the street. Ground lamb for a casserole? Go to the Publix Supermarket two blocks away. Need a Yellow Fever vaccination? You have a choice of doctors in easy walking distance.

Compare that with Andes in the Catskills where a dentist, ground lamb, or exotic vaccination would necessitate a lengthy trek by car to Kingston, Oneonta, or Albany. Sarasota also has pizza delivery and ice cream trucks.

What they don't have in Sarasota is wild animals. No bears, no turkeys, no deer. The wildest animals in town are tourists from Wisconsin wearing colorful Hawaiian shirts, baggy shorts, and tennis shoes.

According to the *Sarasota Herald-Tribune* newspaper, the last time a bear was seen in that town was February 1953 shortly after Dwight D. Eisenhower was inaugurated (editor's note: bears in Florida do not hibernate; also, the Billboard number one song in February 1953 was Perry Como's "Don't Let the Stars Get in Your Eyes").

The Sarasota bear was around a bee hive on the east side of downtown Sarasota. City authorities, not certain what to do and afraid the ursine visitor would scare away human visitors, asked the Florida governor to call out the National Guard. More than one hundred troops spent a week in town. The bear was never seen again, but local bars were thrilled at the jump in receipts.

One of the most irritating aspects of being in Sarasota is "poop patrol." In the Catskills one's dogs simply run outside to do their business wherever they please. Not so in Sarasota. They have stringent laws against dogs crapping on a neighbor's lawn or even in a park. Those people you see in Sarasota walking around with yellow plastic pails and shovels aren't going to the beach. They are picking up after their dogs.

Do Sarasota's pluses outnumber the minuses? It is hard to say. On the positive side are beaches, great water views, businesses, and people everywhere—no snow, warm temperatures, and low taxes. You also hardly see badly cooked broccoli in restaurants. Negatives are mosquitoes, slow drivers, humidity, and mosquitoes again.

In summary, Sarasota is a nice place to visit, but I wouldn't want to live there … unless I could afford it. [Personal to the *Catskill Tribune* editor-in-chief: why did you cut off my office credit card? I was planning to come home in a month or two or three.]

70. MORE THAN THREE DOZEN DEMOCRATS VIE FOR CATSKILL'S SEAT IN US HOUSE OF REPRESENTATIVES

At last count, thirty-seven individuals are on the June 26, 2018 ballot to select a Democratic candidate to run against the Republican incumbent in Congressional District 19 (CD19). Many local polling places have suggested voters supply their own pens to mark ballots. Apparently, the increased cost of printing the multi-page document has depleted precinct budgets.

The *Catskill Tribune*'s political editor traveled around CD19 to interview some of the lesser known candidates. Finding the candidates was not always an easy task. Our editor discovered that a number of them were not presently domiciled in the district. In six cases, candidates did not even reside in the state. One candidate lived in Italy northeast of Rome.

Everyone interviewed agreed that the race was drawing such a large group of candidates because, as one opined, "that Republican incumbent looks like easy pickings."

Candidate John S. Burroughs, interviewed by phone, lives in Butte, Montana, and is proud to have been a member of the Peoples Out-Of-Work Party before registering in Delaware County as a Democrat. Mr. Burroughs admitted that he has only been in Delaware County once in his life when he stayed at an Airbnb in Andes three months ago, while registering to vote. When asked where exactly the rental was located, he admitted he could not remember. But Mr. Burroughs did recollect that the Airbnb was advertised as a "semi-converted barn" and that it was "very inexpensive." Asked what "semi-converted" meant he said, "No indoor plumbing."

Mr. Burroughs was refreshingly frank about his reasons for wanting to hold public office: "I need a paying job and being a member of the US House of Representatives means big bucks. The salary is $174,000 a year, more than I've made my whole life. In two years in office, I can bank enough to live in Montana for a long, long time without lifting a finger. I spent hours at a computer in our local library researching congressional races throughout the country looking for one I fit. The New York CD19 contest looked not bad. Then I found that some guy named Burroughs had been a big deal in the area in the nineteenth century. Bingo! I figured I'd be a shoe-in with name recognition and all. CD19 went from a "maybe" on my list of possibilities to #1. When I get elected. I plan to visit Andes again before I head to Washington D.C. to get sworn in. Then I'll head back to Butte and wait for the checks to roll in. I checked and the House of Representatives has direct deposit."

When asked if he had ever held elective office, Mr. Burroughs thought a bit before admitting he had not. But he did want voters to know he once had been called to jury duty. However, because the person on trial was his brother, he was dismissed.

A second interviewed candidate, Judith Collins, lives in Hudson. Her public service résumé includes serving on her high school prom committee. "I've always wanted to have a well-paid job where I didn't have to be really good in mathematics or science or know a lot. Being in Congress is just the ticket."

Queried about previous jobs and experiences that would make

her an attractive candidate, Ms. Collins talked about working as a shampooer in a unisex hair salon in Hudson. "I watched everything and learned how to dry hair to look terrific. I would have no trouble fitting in with those blow-dried Congressmen and I certainly would look much more attractive than they do. I'd be the most attractive US Rep ever."

By chance, a third candidate also was a resident of Hudson, having moved there from near Dallas, Texas, two years ago. Freddie Fender, a flamboyant exotic dancer, carefully explained that his main reasons for seeking higher office were "to promote more diversity and tolerance" in the world. "We especially need more women in government." When it was pointed out that he was male, Mr. Fender replied, "You should see me in drag. When I dance, I am absolutely gorgeous. Those fuddy duddies in the House will certainly have their consciousness raised."

Five other candidates were located. One lived in a trailer park in Island Grove in northern Florida, which, the candidate emphasized in a telephone conversation, had been home to rock and roll legend, Bo Diddly, for many years. The candidate said she had been in New York City on a high school trip in the 1970s and was looking forward to returning to live there if elected. When it was pointed out that CD19 had nothing to do with New York City, the candidate hung up. The other four candidates all lived in CD19 but refused to speak with our reporter. Most candidates could not be found at all.

Remarkably, our editor turned up evidence suggesting Russian trolls had entered three fictitious candidates in the CD19 race, hoping to confuse voters. The three suspect candidates are Georgina Washington, Thomasina Jefferson, and Billie Clinton. Addresses for the three are recorded as street numbers 38, 40, and 42 on

Smirnoff Boulevard in Woodstock. Neither that street nor any-one with those names could be found in Woodstock directories, though local papers and social media contained numerous paeans of support.

Recognizing the likelihood that Russians were seeking to influ-ence our local election, the *Catskill Tribune*'s editor called election officials in Delhi and left a phone message to that effect. Two days later someone from the Delhi office called back and left an en-quiry on the *Catskill Tribune*'s answering machine asking that we return the call and provide the name of the bridge in Woodstock under which the trolls were living.

71. ARKVILLE ASTROLOGIST ANNOUNCES AMENITY FOR THOSE SEEKING DAILY DIRECTION

The latest business to set up shop in the western Catskills features astrologist André Carlo Royale. Following a Business Association of Roxbury mixer at a local bar-restaurant where Mr. Royale introduced himself to the community, the astrologist sat down with the *Catskill Tribune*'s business reporter to talk about the art of astrology and what he can offer local residents.

Mr. Royale moved to Arkville on the second of April, which, as he noted, "was as cold as the dark side of Neptune." Long a proponent of living off both the land and the generosity of people who availed themselves of his astrological prognostications, Mr. Royale set up a camp near Dry Brook Ridge south from Arkville. He was quick to point out that he did not require a trove of material items to live: "I only need a clear sky, an internet hookup, and access to an ATM; also, a small solar set-up to charge my battery-operated devices. Oh, and a large heated tent with a propane tank for cooking."

Mr. Royale comes to us from the foothills of the southern Cascade Mountains near the small town of Shasta in northern California. He seemed somewhat embarrassed to admit, "I had quite a following out there. Lots of those left-coast people read my online blog every day and many also received a personalized message. They particularly loved my relying on dietary science to help them chart their lives."

Mr. Royale emphasized, "My extraordinary astrological abilities are a gift for which I cannot accept checks. Those wishing to offer cash or credit cards are indulged."

When asked how he managed to garner a living wage and how he found his way to Arkville, Mr. Royale explained: "I received a modest inheritance from an aunt who had spent her life in the Cascades in the town of Klamath Glen. She invented a motorized Ouija Board that ran on batteries. When she died, she left me the patent, her bank account, and her proto-type board, which I use to guide my own life. About two years ago, the Ouija Board told me to go find Roxbury, which I did. After more than eighteen months, however, I found out it was Roxbury, New York, not Roxbury, Connecticut, that I should have been seeking. I immediately headed for the Empire State.

"While I was passing through Arkville on the Trailways bus in early April, my Ouija Board planchette turned itself on and was jumping around in my backpack. I figured I was in the right place, so I disembarked. I actually never made it to downtown Roxbury, but it turns out the bus didn't go there anyway."

When asked where he studied astrology and dietary science, Mr. Royale said, "Berkeley … sort of. My parents thought I was enrolled at the University of California in the late 1960s, but I was actually hanging out on the streets of San Francisco learning my trade.

"It turns out I have a genius for astrology. And I did audit several food science classes at Berkeley. Had I been enrolled, I would have received A's. I was a great student."

Mr. Royale presently is fine-tuning his charts and intends to go public with his Catskills astrology web page in a few weeks. According to Mr. Royale, "The Cascade Mountains and the Catskill Mountains aren't all that different, so retooling things for this locale is not difficult. I've met a lot of people and already several dozen have signed up. Because of the need here in Arkville, I'm adding a new service: reading fortunes from bent and crushed beer cans. It's like reading tea leaves, but requires more skill."

At the close of our interview, the colorful astrologist asked if I would like him to read my chart and offer some advice for the next day. I acceded and Mr. Royale expertly scanned my credit card with an iPhone. For my reading he asked for the date, place, and time I was born, which I provided.

The next morning, I found his email in my inbox. It read:

"Libra—Watch your step before noon! Take extra care to avoid any malodorous messes you may encounter. Afternoon is a good time to clean your shoes and put your life in order. Enhance your diet this evening by ingesting liquids containing the chemical CH_3CH_2OH; stay away from green plants of the species Brassica oleracea that have stalks and feature high dietary fiber. Enjoy your day!"

I thought that was great advice. Then I remembered that in the course of our earlier conversation, I had mentioned to Mr. Royale that in the next morning I was making a trip to a local dairy to interview the farmhands and then intended to have dinner and drinks at the very same restaurant in Roxbury where our interview was taking place. I might also have mentioned that I'm not a broccoli fan.

72. LOCAL BUSINESS HOPES TO SQUASH UNWANTED ROBO TELEPHONE CALLS

An epidemic of computer-generated telephone calls has hit the western Catskills. We've all experienced the intrusive nature of the robo calls. You've just sat down at four o'clock in the afternoon to enjoy a cocktail and read the *Catskill Tribune* when the telephone rings. The call is a dire warning that without purchasing a medical alert bracelet your life is in grave danger.

The phone rings again. This time it is a call from the (fake) Internal Revenue Service asking you to buy a cash card to pay an outstanding tax lien or you might have to sell your home. No sooner have you sat back down when the phone rings a third time with an offer to enjoy a free weekend in Kingston, New York—only a credit card number is required.

According to the New York Times, Americans received 3.4 billion such calls in April 2018 from more than 200,000 telephone scammers. The federal government's National Do Not Call Registry is a colossal failure.

Scammers now use computer technology to mask their real calling number and make it appear that they are calling from a local number, hoping you are more likely to answer and listen to the sales pitch. For instance, your phone may indicate the call comes from a number sporting an 845 prefix (eastern Catskills); but the call might actually come from somewhere in Uzbekistan.

Fed up with telephone abuse, a coalition of local investors hired a team of Onteora Central School student techies to come up with a way to screen spam calls, one uniquely suited to the Catskills. The result is an app called RoboPlop that the inventors and investors hope to sell to Android and iPhone users, as well as to telephone companies that provide landlines here in the Catskills.

RoboPlop's advertising logo features a dairy cow pooping on a phone. Using a special paper, the ad firm providing the sales brochure for RoboPlop made the logo "come alive" when the brochure was moved. The plop appears to actually land on the telephone. Investors greeted the brochure at a launch meeting with great glee.

Telephone users with the app on their cellular phone or who use it with their landline can opt to have all robo calls automatically "killed," that is, transferred to a computer. The computer then discerns the actual number from which the call was made and for the next twenty-four hours inundates it with repeated calls featuring the sound of flatulent cow defecation.

Another RoboPlop option also intended to irritate telemarketers is to select a common Catskill noise that can be used to bombard the scammers with repeated calls. Among the growing list of options are: (1) the sound of spring peepers that quickly escalates in volume to an ear-splitting level; (2) the much less soothing yapping of hunting coyotes followed by the ominous message, "they are coming for you ... tonight;" (3) a jug band incessantly playing an instrumental version of "My Heart Will Go On," the Céline Dion's song from the movie, Titanic; and, (4) a never-ending recording of the Roxbury fire station's noon whistle.

Creative users of the app can also record their own message to be played back to scammers. Among suggestions are political diatribes;

information about investing in a Nigerian gold mine; a chance to receive a new generation medical alert accessory (an anklet that is actually a tattoo); and a robotic voice repeating "press 1 to hear more; press 2 to end this call; press 3 to rot in hell."

An answering message intended for those scam calls originating in the United States, as opposed to abroad, announces: "You have reached the Internal Revenue Service's 'Please Audit Me' hot line. We have recorded the number you are calling from and will arrange your audit soon. There is no charge for this service."

The RoboPlop team expects to eventually market their product throughout the country.